"Mrs. B[...] [inter]rupted, "perhaps it would not be out of place to mention that I was educated in a convent in France. When I did wrong, I was whipped. I do not believe it did me any lasting harm; on the contrary, it is likely that at the very least it taught me manners."

Even now, as the Captain sat in his office at Norfolk, the memory sent a shiver up his spine. The sheer command of the woman!

So the Captain had overridden Sandy's objections, Amanda had applied, and she had been accepted. There was nothing to worry about, really. She had always been a good girl.

Other Books by
Blue Moon Authors

AMANDA

TIMOTHY TAYLOR

BLUE MOON

BLUE MOON BOOKS, INC. NEW YORK

First Blue Moon Edition 1993
First Printing 1993

ISBN 1-56201-036-0

Published by Blue Moon Books, Inc.
PO Box 1040
Cooper Station, NY 10276

Manufactured in the United States of America

To my wife Barbara, an invaluable ally in the researching of this book.

Part 1

The Cane

Amanda opened her notebook carefully so that the letter wouldn't show. She wanted to read it again—desperately—but she dared not attract the attention of her classmates, or even worse, that of her teacher Miss Markham. She knew full well that it was not just the words, the plans of her dear Raymond that were contraband—it was what would be by inference revealed about her. Amanda knew that she had transgressed. She was afraid of the punishment that could ensue.

Madame Girard had made it clear on the first day of their attendance at her academy: "I do not divorce life and knowledge; your teachers will be your instructors not only in their respective fields, but they will also try to guide you toward the moral values we expect at our school."

Amanda remembered that speech very well; she had sat quietly with the other newcomers to Madame Girard's Academy, and she had felt the pride that comes with being one of the elect. Leaving home had been a relief rather than a trauma; she was an only child, between two parents. The rigorous standards and code of discipline at the school had not frightened her; she felt at home from the beginning. Still, her quiet childhood on a Virginia farm, her love of cinematic fantasy, the aloofness that she had inherited from her father—none of these had prepared her for a closely ordered life among numerous girls her own age. By and large, she had done well this school year—yet there was only one week remaining, and among her classmates she did not have a single true friend.

Amanda looked up at Miss Markham but her head was bent over her papers. I could tell her of anything, Amanda thought, but this.

I have to decide today.

The notebook lay flat and closed before her. Her mind struck its blank wall and wandered off into the cinematic world of her childhood, where she was always director, cameraman, and star.

She began the narration in her mind: Today is June tenth, nineteen seventy. We are in the red free study room of Madame Girard's Academy, located a few miles north of Philadelphia. It is a select establishment for smart privileged young ladies between the ages of sixteen and eighteen. This room recalls precisely the old fashioned sitting room it once was— chandeliered expanse, ornate carving in the door, heavy carpet in anticipation of a servant's soundless step. I'm the blonde girl near the center, sitting on the long side of a rectangular table. Seven other girls sit about the room, displaying various degrees of diligence. All of them are in my grade except for Ginny, who sits at a small table in the corner, maintaining her upper class distance. I've noticed Ginny giving me a sad, secretive smile sometimes, when she thinks

I'm not looking, but whenever I try to smile back, her face turns to stone. Yet I like her taut, thin face; I know I have nothing to fear from her. It's Sherry Paxton I must watch. She sits diagonally across from me, and being a Main Line girl, she would look down on me if she could. Unfortunately she is six inches shorter than my five-seven—a lack she makes up for, with interest, in the waistline. She pretends to feel that I am inferior, because my father is a career military man—"in service"—she says with a sniff, as though the Captain of a destroyer was a butler!

She doesn't know that it is my father's romantic patriotism that brought him into the Navy—not the pittance of a Captain's pay. He could have lived easily on the Beasley fortune—but he chose military career, just as I will make my own place in life.

Meanwhile, her father is but the idle son of a garbage entrepreneur; clean hands, indeed! I can feel sorry for Sherry, for no one will compare her to a fair Duchess of Alba (ah Raymond!) yet I must be vigilant, for her jealousy could be my undoing.

Most of all, however, I must consider Miss Markham. She is sitting quietly at her desk now, glasses on, going over her reports. I like Miss Markham; she is pretty, with a softness even her upswept hair and granny glasses cannot disguise. She listens to me when I talk, when I talk of all those things a girl might tell her mother, if her mother would listen. Mother—she tells me to call her Sandy—is cold as a beach in Autumn, glittering for a moment at a party, but never giving. I don't touch my mother, except in a public manner, for display—the Captain's wife and their lovely daughter! I don't touch Miss Markham either, for she is my teacher, but sometimes . . .

Miss Markham teaches appreciation of English Literature. One day she was reading "The Highwayman" aloud and I saw a tear form behind the gleam of her glasses. In my silent dreams at night Miss Markham is my sister. I can hear Madame Girard's voice, "Instructor . . . moral values." I know that if my teacher finds the letter my fingers tremble over, she will turn me in to Madame Girard. She won't have any other choice. I mustn't cry.

If only I had the safety of my own room to hide! But we have double rooms, and I have Michelle.

* * *

Captain Beasley sat in his office at the Norfolk Navy Base, musing over what he would write to Amanda. Ever since she was a little girl he had written her letters—when she was very small he had held her on his lap while she read them. It was a way for this quiet man to express himself, and Amanda had always loved the letters. Not that she ever wrote back.

Maybe someday she'll write a screenplay, he thought, but that's the most I can expect. Probably the only writing she'll do is pencil in a few lines on the script.

He imagined her in the future, in Hollywood, and as always it felt as though a huge lump of fear and pride had formed in his chest. Amanda had always loved the movies and it scared him to think of how beautiful she was now. He had kept her somewhat sheltered, for he knew she had that ability that all great actresses have—some combination of sex appeal and charisma that drew everyone's attention to her.

I don't think she knows she has it yet, but it's just a matter of time. First there will be a man—he felt a tremor in his heart but pushed his thoughts on—

and then there will be a long distance phone call, "Daddy I got a job in Hollywood! I've got a part in a movie! I haven't got an apartment yet, but you can write me care of the studio, here let me give you the address . . ." Then we'll read in the newspapers about how she got discovered—on God I don't know if I can bear it.

I'm glad she's been at Madame Girard's this year, and she'll go back next year—it will probably be the last peaceful time of her life. I like the way the place is run, like a taut ship—there's just that one thing that worries me, and got the first real spark out of Sandy in years. Maybe I should have listened to her—but the school was her idea in the first place!

*   *   *

Perhaps it started with the towels, Amanda thought. There were showers and a large bathroom at the end of the hall, but each room had its own sink with a small medicine cabinet (there was a mirror on the door, but what Amanda really liked was the full length mirror on the inside of the door to the bedroom closet). Above the sink to the left were two towel racks.

Amanda, a tall girl, had naturally placed her towel on the top rack in the course of her unpacking. That was eight months ago, but it still hurt to recall the nasty shock she got the next day.

"Your roommate will not be arriving until tomorrow," Madame Girard had told her. "Her name is Michelle Hamilton and she is coming from Dublin— I understand the delay is due to a dense fog over the airport. I do hope you will make her welcome when she arrives."

Hamilton. Amanda was sure that Michelle's father

was *the* Roger Hamilton, the famous English thriller writer who lived in Ireland for tax reasons. She had never read any of his books, but several had been made into movies, and she had seen every one of those. One series featured an anonymous, world weary secret agent played by the aging but still devastating actor Spike Arlen. Amanda would quiver in her seat when Arlen would suddenly explode with furious bursts of violence or passion. She had no trouble at all imagining herself as the treacherous heroine who inspired such passion.

Amanda fell asleep peacefully that night, thinking a little of her father, dreaming her way into old movies, looking forward to meeting Michelle . . .

That was the first, last, and only peaceful night Amanda spent at Madame Girard's.

Michelle breezed in the next day with a flippant greeting for Amanda; she admitted her famous ancestry in a—to Amanda—affected accent; she unpacked quickly and sloppily; and she walked over to the towel racks, took down Amanda's towel and put it on the lower one, and lofted her own to the top.

It was such a blow to Amanda's sense of propriety, yet at the same time such a petty action that Amanda could think of nothing to say.

Things had gone downhill from there. Michelle was a voluble talker (though of little substance, Amanda thought), while Amanda had an air of quietude, of repose around her. Their enmity was shallow—there had been no direct, painful confrontation—but there was no trust. Amanda felt choked in Michelle's presence, wondering if the short redhead was doing things purposely to annoy her, or whether she just had no consideration.

Sometimes Amanda wished she could have broken the deadlock early with a few well chosen words

(Could we be friends? We know so little of each other) but the words did not come, and now . . . Now it was too late.

The night would come soon. She had to decide now.

* * *

Captain Beasley had laid down his pen. He was thinking back to that first meeting with Madame Girard . . .

He and Sandy had come to the nearly deserted school last summer. A secretary had ushered them past a frosted door that carried the inscription, Mme. Girard, Directrice. The Captain had smiled at the French title, and then he saw the woman.

She wore a single diamond, gleaming at her throat. Her dress was elegant, black, and decollete. Her face had stood the test of fifty summers—and expected to see fifty more.

The total effect was awesome. The Captain realized instantly why she had retained the bi-syllabic French form of address. A mere Miss could never do justice to such a woman.

The Captain's lady was less impressed, although it is possible that a worm of envy may have clouded her judgment.

It *was* Mrs. Beasley's influence that had led them to this preliminary interview concerning Amanda's enrollment. There were many hurdles to cross before that possible event, and this was only one of them. mere twenty girls in each class were accepted per year. Both academic and financial standards were rigorous. The exclusivity had appealed to Sandy— not least because of the status symbol it had become among the elite society of the eastern seaboard. It was quite a coup to be able to mention, casually, "Why, my daughter's away at Madame Girard's, don't you know?"

Now, trying to meet that lady's eyes (which stared at her, Sandy fancied, as though she were merely an overweight schoolgirl guilty of some obscure sin) Mrs. Beasley began to abdicate her former position. Unfortunately, she could see at a glance that her husband, previously unconvinced, was rapidly changing his position—a change that had a direct relation to the approval so apparent in his eyes as he gazed at Madame Girard.

I suppose there must be some naval term for it, Sandy thought. Turning about the squadron, he would say. Taking over the enemy's territory. And we are enemies, aren't we, Teddy boy? Twenty years and what do I have? A man who dreams of commanding a frigate, while he's actually spent the last ten years on staff duty. A daughter who doesn't speak to me, on whose behalf I'm trying to deal with this French autocrat. Better Amanda should stay home—and then suddenly Sandy realized that for the first time in years she had relapsed (if only in her mind) to the Yiddish idiom of her childhood— that she had tried so hard to forget.

"What made you decide to open your school, Madame?" Ted was asking, like a little boy, Sandy thought.

"Seven years ago, Captain, when I was living in London, I was surprised to discover that I had inherited this house. I am, as you may know, distantly related to the Philadelphia Girards, though of course this connection predates our famous Stephen's trip to the New World. It seems that the lady who lived here spent considerable solicitor's fees trying to find me. Her qualifications for an heir were possibly rather eccentric. She sought a woman, related by blood, with the surname Girard, who lived alone and was successful in her own right. This, of course, was much like the lady herself. Eventually it was determined, without my knowledge, that I satisfied the requirements.

"Why a girls' school? I had this house, the means, knowledge and experience in the teaching field. I also feel a certain tradition, a respect for classical virtues that, alas, seemed to be missing in the American scene.

"I am a realist. I have no desire to change the world in sweeping terms. But I thought that if I could guide a few select young ladies, my life would not be wholly without purpose."

She must have it memorized, thought Sandy, but it *is* impressive. Yet I wonder about this living alone.

"Did you never marry, Miss Girard?" Sandy asked.

"In truth I prefer to be called Madame" (here Captain Beasley smiled slightly, which smile was not missed by his wife) "for the simple reason that I am no Miss in search of a man. I have never married, and now I have reached a point in my life where I feel most comfortable with my own company."

Madame leaned forward slightly to push her chair back. Ted felt a powerful but unreasonable desire to caress the white slope of her bosom.

"Would you like me to show you around the school?"

"By all means."

They examined the classrooms, the red free study room, the girls' bedrooms upstairs. The innate luxuriousness of the house tended to soften the scholarly atmosphere. The only alterations the Captain could see were on the second and third floors, where partitions had divided vast bedrooms into the girls' apartments.

It transpired that Madame Girard actually lived in a small cottage on the grounds, that in former times had been rented to a young college professor. The Beasleys discovered this while standing near the stables, looking out over a verdant pasture, equipped in one corner with ring and cavaletti.

The Captain slowly turned full circle, taking in the view. Stables, pastures, cottage, mansion—Gothic spires?

"Is that . . . ?" he paused, trying to recall.

"Yes, the Bryn Athyn Cathedral. In their pursuit of God's perfection, their work is as yet unfinished."

Most people would have said that flippantly, thought the Captain, as he continued to gaze at the great Gothic tower. Yet in those words I heard the first humble tones of the day. She is very interesting.

The group walked slowly back to the iron gate that would return the visitors to a less extravagant world. The Captain mulled over his excellent impressions; Sandy felt out of her depth, in a situation that she couldn't control. She did not want Amanda to go to school here, yet she could think of no clear reason for her change of heart, nor could she imagine a worthwhile objection, until Ted raised a question.

"It is a self contained world you have here, Madame," he began, with great deliberation, "and I am impressed. The substitution of grace, scholarship and horses for television, marijuana, and cars is to my mind an advantageous exchange. Yet I have commanded a ship on the high seas, and I know from experience that men in this kind of confined environment can become quite restless. Now my experience with women is limited; I have only two ladies in my life"—here he smiled at Sandy, who returned it, perfunctorily—"but even that number can be quite a handful. Tell me Madame, how do you keep things running smoothly when you have forty vibrant young ladies under one roof?"

"In the first place," Madame Girard replied, "We try to minimize differences. The girls all wear the same outfit of white blouse and dark blue skirt. This is the outward symbol of the fact that each girl will be treated according to her merits—and no young lady may attempt to impress another with the irrelevant fact that her father can supply her with twelve different dresses for each separate week.

"Then we have the equestrian sports you mentioned. Physical exercise is a great reliever of tensions. And yet I still have not completely answered your question."

"You are correct. As an officer, I believe in the value of discipline among men. I must confess, however, that with young ladies I am at a loss."

"I too believe in the value of discipline. If we are to instruct, we must have order. In this particular case, I have found it most effective to return to the time honored practice of corporal punishment. We use the cane."

There was a sudden, intense silence, and then Mrs. Beasley's voice broke out, loud and strained, "Jesus Christ! That's the most stupid and barbaric thing I've ever heard! If you think—"

"Mrs. Beasley," Madame Girard interrupted, "perhaps it would not be out of place to mention that I was educated in a convent in France. When I did wrong, I was whipped. I do not believe it did me any lasting harm; on the contrary, it is likely that at the very least it taught me manners."

Even now, as the Captain sat in his office at Norfolk, the memory sent a shiver up his spine. The sheer command of the woman!

So the Captain had overridden Sandy's objections, Amanda had applied, and she had been accepted. There was nothing to worry about, really. She had always been a good girl.

* * *

Amanda looked around the room without turning her head, straining her peripheral vision. Then she flipped the page of her notebook and saw her name. It was boldly written with a red felt tip pen. She knew every word of the letter that followed, yet it was only by seeing the red of his ink, of his blood, that it became real . . .

They had met by chance three weeks before. Amanda had tired of the deliberate motions that were to make her a lady. She *was* a lady! She was also a girl, an adventurous girl, and she needed to run. She slipped through the iron gates after breakfast that cool May morning, wearing her skirt and blouse and high heels. She slid the shoes off, clutched them in her hands, and *ran* for the end of the driveway. Wild exhilaration bubbled up in her as her stockinged feet raced over the gray asphalt. She spun around the corner on to the main road, running in unrestrained joy, as a motorcycle roared past her going the other way. After a time she slowed to a walk, laughing to herself, her heart pounding, her breasts heavy and alive against her heaving chest.

I could sing, Amanda thought, I could sing with my body tingling like this, and when I go back I'll carry this feeling with me and tonight I'll take a shower and touch myself and . . .

"Hello!" The cheery masculine voice behind her caused Amanda to spin around with a start.

She collected herself quickly, observing the man: black hair, a Latin look, white teeth in a grin.

"Hello," she said—the voice of a lady who wants for nothing.

"I am an expert chessplayer, and a hopeful playwright," he said, "interesting facts, but difficult to believe, or even understand, when hurled above the thunder of a powerful motorcycle. Rounding the curve back there, I passed a vision of Beauty and I knew I could never forgive myself if I did not seek a second look. So I pushed my machine into the woods, and I ran down the path of your footsteps. I was prepared to be disappointed. I see now I was wrong in thinking of a Vision of Beauty. Visions are ephemeral. Your beauty if real.

"My name is Raymond Navarre. What is yours?" He extended his hand with the introduction.

"Amanda," she said, sailing on the flow of his words, and she started to put out her hand—only to feel her self possession vanish, as she realized she still held her shoes! Should she perform the awkward maneuver of putting them on? She looked at Raymond in confusion.

"It doesn't matter," he said. "We don't need to shake hands."

As he spoke, he reached forward with both hands, and caught her wrists. She trembled in his grasp, but did not try to move away. Nor did he try to pull her toward him. He just held her firmly, and looked into her eyes, blue like the summer sky. And then his eyes seemed to read her face, a feather touch along the lines of her high cheekbones, a tickle down her aristocratic nose, a gossamer kiss for her full lips. His eyes lingered there, and then he did begin to pull her toward him, as his own body came closer and his face blotted out the sun. Their lips touched, and held for a second, and then he let go of her wrists to put his arms around her in a gentle embrace. After a moment he put his hands on her shoulders and guided her back a pace.

"If you would lean on me, Amanda, I'm sure you could get your shoes on."

She smiled and leaned against his side while he put an arm around her shoulders. Soon the shoes were on and they were walking slowly together, heading back to the iron gates.

Amanda made it back to the school without incident that time, although it was against the rules for the girls to wander off the property unchaperoned. She flouted the rule again and again in the ensuing weeks—she had had a taste of magic and her heart craved more.

Dear Amanda—her eyes flashed around the room for a last check; Miss Markham was busy with her papers, Sherry was doodling aimlessly, the other girls were too far away to present a danger.

She ducked her head and began to read.

Dear Amanda,

I will come for you because I love you. I will take you because I want you. Two nights from now, I want you to look out at 3:00 A.M. I will be there, but only you can open the window.

Let me explain, quietly, what has happened. When I came here to rest in the shadow of the cathedral, I didn't know when—if ever—my play (The Bass Place) would be seen.

Yesterday, Benjamin Hillery (my producer-mortician friend) called me and said that he had a theater for us if we could set up sharp and fast for a limited run. There are only three weeks to cast and rehearse, and in view of our lack of funds, I will have to direct it myself.

In other words, I must go to New York.

Two days is all I can wait, while I remember the sweetness of each and every kiss.

I know where your room is.

I know where your window is.

I will come for you.

Love,
Raymond

Amanda never knew how her face, usually so peaceful, had flashed like a semaphore while she read the letter. She had gone up and down on the rollercoaster Raymond had created, and when she was finished all she could think of was the last sweet kiss they had shared.

It was two days ago, the day he had given her the letter. Amanda was ready to leave, fearful she would be missed. Raymond had other plans. He caught her arm, and said jokingly, (though the grip on her arm was no joke) "I propose, in honor of the esteemed Madame Defarge, excuse me, Madame Girard, that we enjoy one last French kiss."

Then, both hands on her arms now, he had drawn her to him, his grip powerful but his lips tender, light and caressing until he felt her response, then his mouth opened and his tongue rushed in to claim his victory. His hands were on her back now, pressing and sliding down, down over her behind and then sinking like talons into the softness of her upper thighs, vulnerable flesh above her stocking tops, protected only by one simple layer of skirt. He held her with such force that she was almost raised from the ground, helpless against him, her mouth plundered and open, her body perfectly safe in his arms . . .

"Amanda."

The sound was like a switch clicking in her brain as memory's glorious vision was abruptly shut off.

In its place was silence, and the awful realization that everyone in the room was staring at her. She didn't have to look around to know that Madame Girard stood behind her—where she could see the letter! Without any thought Amanda slammed the notebook shut. This second sound cracked the charged silence, and now the schoolgirls were tittering, laughing as the blood rose in Amanda's face.

Madame Girard gestured behind her, and the room was silent once more. Amanda dared not look around, nor could she bear to see the faces of her peers. She turned her eyes to Miss Markham. Her teacher's face was set in professional guise, but her brown eyes were trying to send a message. Amanda's heightened senses suddenly understood—Miss Markham knew! That was why she had never said anything when Amanda was late for class (so many times!)—and somewhere in her subconscious mind Amanda had known she would not. Here today, she certainly knew what Amanda was reading, but she had said nothing. Those soft brown eyes—Amanda loved her then—but the face hard; it was all over now. Miss Markham could protect her no longer. Amanda gave her teacher, her sister a tremulous smile—and then she tightened the control over her face and turned to look at Madame Girard.

Madame stood wearing a long, high necked gown of a deep brown color, broken only by a small necklace of pearls. She spoke in a voice like a November wind.

"Amanda, you will come with me now to my office." She looked over Amanda's head. "Miss Markham, carry on with your duties, but please come down to my office for a visit when this study period ends."

"Yes, Madame," Miss Markham answered.

Amanda had no time to think of her teacher, for immediately she had to follow Madame out of the room. She felt caught in some tortuous nightmare. Madame seemed enormous, in her dirgelike color of Autumn, and it was all Amanda could do to keep step. She dreamed she was a child, dragged tearfully but inevitably along—but really this had never happened before! She remembered herself as a little girl, sitting in her father's lap, listening to sea stories.

Amanda fought for a grip. Hold your head up, she told herself. You're not a child, no you're a girl, you're a woman no don't cry don't cry your father can't help you now you must do it yourself—hold your head up, be *brave*—

Amanda sucked in her breath and let it out very slowly—her fingers sank into her precious notebook so hard that her knuckles showed white—but she held herself erect as a young lady should, while Madame Girard shut the office door behind her.

The Directrice passed by Amanda and seated herself behind her desk. She looked at the girl, standing there so straight, holding her notebook, waiting. Madame had a sudden vision of a young bird climbing out of its nest, wings fluttering on the edge of first flight. The vision sent a gust of sympathy through her, a sentiment that she did not allow to reach her eyes.

Her voice was strong, but not unkind. "You may sit down, Amanda."

That was not what Amanda wanted to hear. She needed the vertical posture of her body to hold up her resolve. She had a sudden flash of folding in on herself, knees buckling ignominiously.

Then she heard a voice inside her head, a new voice, that of a woman who knows her own mind. It was faint, like a far off tinkling piano, but Amanda heard it, and hearkened to whom she would become. The voice said, It does not matter how Madame Girard treats you, nor even what sort of woman she is. She may be good, or evil, or shading anywhere in between, but she is singular. You are distinct from her, from your parents, even from Raymond. Take control, Amanda. Your fear is real, yes, your pain will be real—accept it as the choice of a woman in love—or hide your head like a child, call your father to the rescue, close your window . . .

Amanda thought of every muscle as she sat down, with utmost correctness.

"Let us proceed to the first order of business. Give me the letter."

A pause.

"No."

Amanda had never defied anyone before in her life. Her fingertips burned where they pressed down on her notebook. She sat very still, so tight that her body sought release in an involuntary shiver—suppressed at great cost.

It was with utter astonishment that she beheld Madame Girard's slow, but wide and genuine smile.

"I understand. I too have been in love."

Amanda was more disconcerted than ever. Madame seemed to know far too much.

"Let us take another tack. You are, I'm sure, familiar with Poe?" Madame waited for the girl's nod before continuing. "It was my native country that first appreciated his genius. For myself, I have always been fascinated by his great detective, C. Au-

24

guste Dupin. I used to walk the streets of Paris, feeling his nervous presence beside me. Perhaps he is with me still?

"In the style of my literary friend, I believe I might hazard a few deductions."

Madame's eyes were clear now as she looked at Amanda. There was still a faint smile on her face.

"First let me dispense with one of your fears. I will honor your desire to retain the privacy of your correspondence. In any case it is not necessary. Your very refusal serves only to confirm my thesis; while tending to disprove a certain rumor, which I will get to later.

"The basic facts are these. First, your teachers have reported that your schoolwork has deteriorated in recent weeks. Not to an alarming degree, to be sure, but noticeable. No doubt this would go unremarked in a large public school, but here we try to keep in close touch with all our young ladies. Secondly, your manners have become affected with a certain—disinterest, shall we say. Miss O'Rourke, your Mathematics teacher, remarks that on at least one occasion she greeted you in the hall and received no reply. She knows that no malice was intended, but she was disturbed to see you rushing by, as if in another world. Thirdly, while you were formerly punctual, I have heard reports that you no longer find it necessary to arrive on time—to *one* of your classes. That is a point I will return to."

Amanda felt the weight of these accusations, none of which she could deny, but felt shame for only one. Miss Markham—

"What could have brought about this change in you?" Madame Girard sliced neatly into Amanda's thoughts, her great black eyes penetrating like a hawk's.

25

This time Amanda could not meet her gaze. The guilt she felt over involving Miss Markham robbed her of strength.

"It was necessary to consider drugs as a cause; however, that possibility could be dismissed almost at once. Drugs are a violation of the body, cutting a chemical swath across the rhythms of your life. A mere glance shows you to be in the full bloom of health—glowing with youth, and beauty."

This last was delivered softly, like a cat approaching a mousehole.

"There is only one opiate I know of that produces this combination of a blooming self and a careless concern for others. It is called—love.

"Look up at me Amanda."

Hard black eyes stared into the soft mist of tear shrouded blue.

"You have been seeing a man, secretly, outside of school. Is that correct?"

The answer came softer than a whisper. "Yes."

"Do not look away. Consider what you have done. Your parents have entrusted you to us for your education, and also for your health and safety. We do not put guards on the gate. It is expected that our girls will stay within the grounds, not that they will endanger themselves in pursuit of selfish adventures.

"This is, at least, something you must have considered. However, there is a larger problem, of which you may not be aware. There is a growing tension in this school. Your actions have not gone unnoticed by the other students—especially your continual tardiness to Miss Markham's classes. Large rumors have built up from these small beginnings—some of them had reached my ears, which is why I came for you today.

"It is the nature of the human animal to seek answers. When these are sought through the medium of gossip the result is generally touched with malice. To be plain, the rumor I heard is that you are 'getting away with it' due to an 'unnatural' friendship with Miss Markham."

Amanda started up, amazed, but she made no sound except a sudden intake of breath. All the words left her head at this sudden turn.

Madame gave a short laugh. "Is it not astonishing? But I did not bring you here to listen to gossip."

The Directrice's voice hardened. "This is what you must hear."

It comes now, thought Amanda. As if from far away, she heard the notes of a tinkling piano—suddenly overriden by the harsh tenor of her Directrice.

"You have broken the trust we placed in you. Your thoughtless behavior has set a bad example for all of our young ladies. You have taken advantage of your friendship with a fine, though perhaps overly sentimental teacher. In so doing, you have allowed her reputation to be impugned, and her effectiveness in the classroom, diminished.

"In summation, you have torn a hole in the fabric of our society. It must be mended."

The black eyes searched her face.

"You must be punished."

Amanda wanted desperately to cry but couldn't; she felt an ocean of shame rolling over her and saw no escape—didn't deserve to escape. She shivered with fear because she knew with a shuddering certainty that Madame Girard was right.

She looked up into the Directrice's harsh face for a long second—then, feeling her eyes blur, Amanda bowed her head.

Madame Girard leaned slightly forward, into the air of Amanda's acceptance.

"You will receive the traditional"—here she paused, until Amanda's features began to tighten—"six strokes with the cane.

"You will go to your room now, and make the prescribed change in clothing. After dinner tonight, at nine o'clock precisely, you will report to Miss Markham's office. She will conduct you to me."

The interview was over. Amanda found herself able to make only one feeble request. "May I have dinner in my room?"

The Directrice was already rising. "No," she answered.

Amanda rose slowly on legs that threatened to fail. Her entire body felt exhausted—only her hands clutching her notebook retained any strength. She moved like a sleepwalker toward the door, wanting only to be gone, to be in her own room. Her hand was on the knob—she barely had the strength to push the door open—and then she was out in the hallway. She started up the stairs to her room, but stopped to rest on the fourth step, holding tight to the banister with one hand. She heard a door open behind her, and turned her head just in time to catch a glimpse of Miss Markham's white face as she disappeared into the Directrice's office. Her teacher was obeying her own summons.

Amanda was too drained to register any emotion. She climbed the stairs slowly to her room, took off her clothes, and went down the hall to take a shower.

* * *

Captain Beasley read over his letter, folded it once and held it tenderly in his hand. The school term would be over in another week; just a few more days and he would be bringing his beautiful daughter home. He smiled, picturing Amanda, and reached for an envelope.

* * *

Amanda stood under the shower, letting the burning spray drench her. She was alone and wanted to stay that way. She wished that she would never have to leave this place of heat and steam, never have to go back to her room, never put on . . .

It doesn't matter, it doesn't matter, I can cry here, she thought, but the tears didn't come for suddenly the image of Miss Markham's white face flashed across her mind.

In an instant the shower had changed to become a hot close prison. She had to escape! She toweled herself roughly, threw on a robe, and ran down the hall to her room.

It was four o'clock in the afternoon. Michelle was gone to her (and Amanda's) last class of the day: French. She would be back at five.

It was a tradition at the Academy that a girl who was to be punished did not have to attend classes for the remainder of the day. She was given time to consider what was in store for her. Only the dinner attendance was mandatory.

Amanda lay prone on the bed, trying to imaging what it would be like when she came down—everyone would know, would watch her like a captive animal . . .

She rolled around on to her back and cried to the empty ceiling, "So what!"

Then her lips curved in a real, but fleeting smile— she propped her head up with both hands behind her neck, and began to think. She had an hour to herself, and she would make the most of her time.

* * *

Miss Markham left the Directrice's office and headed for her English Literature class. Her stride was long, her smile wide, but her eyes did not quite meet those of her students. She talked all through the hour long class, going from high point to high point, while the girls watched and whispered among themselves.

Afterwards, none of the girls could remember a word that Miss Markham had said—but they all remembered her face.

* * *

The piano played softly in the background of her thoughts as Amanda lay on her bed.

Normally when she was alone her thoughts were filled totally with Raymond, his presence blotting out all competition. Now it was different. She could open her notebook, take out his letter and read it over. No one would bother her.

Yet she didn't want to do that yet. Raymond was here, with her, but it seemed as though he was standing to one side, waiting quietly.

Amanda had never had a real sense of herself. She could picture herself, see her image as a camera would, but she never felt herself taking up space, having weight in the play of human affairs. She had always run with the flow, eased around corners by the facts of beauty and money that she took for granted.

Yet now she found herself a stationary figure, about whom other people revolved—or sometimes collided: Miss Markham, her parents, even Madame Girard.

Madame did have power over her—she bowed to

that power, yet part of Madame's strength derived from Amanda's acceptance.

I made a choice in that office when I bowed my head, thought Amanda. I will stay, I will take my punishment, and I will go with Raymond.

It's true that I could become as a child again. I could call my father and he would come for me; he would take me home—and I would never see Raymond again.

I reject this, for I am a woman. Even though no man has broken his way inside of me, I am a woman because I love, because I am loved.

Miss Markham, I see your face dear sister. I used you and now what can I do? I'm glad you will be with me tonight. I'm glad you will see . . . No one else, just you . . .

Daddy, I see you and I love you but I'm not your little girl any more. How can I tell you that I won't see you next week? How can I tell you that I won't be coming home? I'm going to hurt you Daddy, yes I love you I'm going to hurt you . . . I'm going to see a man, a bold man, I'm going to go with him Daddy. I'm going to take off my clothes and lie on my back and he will be over me, I'm going to open my legs for him Daddy, I'll open—

The sound of her own harsh panting breath snapped Amanda out of her waking dream. She realized with a feeling almost of horror that her right hand was buried between her bare legs. She jerked it away, then struggled to close her robe that had fallen open.

Her body screamed in one way, while her mind skittered in another—she desperately sought solid ground and saw the clock hands at four forty-five.

Only fifteen minutes until Michelle would arrive! She hadn't dressed. Her heart skipped a beat and then thumped on, high and hard. She must put on the prescribed clothing. It was black, and it lay hidden at the bottom of her underwear drawer.

Amanda got out of bed and opened the drawer. She put her hand out tentatively, touching scented pastel lace. Suddenly she plunged her hand deep into the drawer, knocking her neat piles awry. Blackness spilled out at the bottom. She took out the black silk panties and laid them on the bed.

She returned to the open drawer and saw the garter belt, coiled darkly. She lifted it out and laid it by the panties.

She returned again to the bureau, moving more slowly this time. Her hand hesitated, almost trembling, before she finally reached out for the delicate black silk stockings. Every girl had such a pair, hidden away. Madame Girard had decreed it. Every girl hoped that she would never have to wear them.

Amanda stared at the splashes of black on her white bedspread.

She knew why she had to wear this garb, a delicate yet shocking evocation of sin. She was an example. For the same reason she must appear at dinner. Every eye would be drawn to the sheen of black silk below her skirt. The image would work on the minds of all.

They could imagine what was in store for her.

Amanda shuddered as she reached for the black garter belt. Just to put it on would mark the beginning of her punishment.

There was still time. She could throw on her normal uniform, rush downstairs and call her father. He would come for her in his big Buick and take her home. She would be safe—and she wouldn't see Raymond; Raymond; Raymond.

Her head drooped and she realized that she was

holding the garter belt so tightly that her knuckles were white. Her breath was loud and shallow.

Why can I not act on my decision? She asked herself silently.

And then she realized, and it was not a nice discovery, that the hardest decisions of life go on and on. They give one no peace and must be fought with as many times as the brain returns to the subject. They have nothing in common with the heroic snap judgements of cinema.

Amanda made herself look beyond nine o'clock. She thought of the night, of her man, of the new morning that would come. She forced herself to begin the physical action she dreaded.

She untied the sash of her robe and shrugged it off, still holding the garter belt in her other hand. She opened the closet door to reveal the full length mirror. She turned to face her reflection as she snapped the garter belt about her slender waist. She reached for the stockings as she sat down on a corner of the bed, still gazing at herself. The silk fit over her toes and slid up her legs. She fastened the garter clasps.

Amanda stood up, still watching, head slightly lowered, mind and eye working only in image, not ideas. She looked at her black framed blondness and her white skin. Black and blonde and white. Black and blonde and white.

She touched the blondness with a delicate finger, then suddenly pulled her hand to one side, as if frightened. Her fingertips trailed across the straps of the garter belt, over her hips and behind her to the bare softness of her buttocks.

She gasped, imagining the cane lashing into her—and then the vision changed abruptly and she was feeling Raymond's hands on her, siding down, holding her, and now her fingers were slyly coming around to the front again, seeking the wetness so evident now—Amanda froze.

Michelle was in the room.

Amanda didn't move. She just stood there, a statue wishing to weep, sensing her roommate behind her and to one side. It seemed as though everything and everyone had snuck up on her today.

Amanda felt powerless and very naked. She wanted to slip on her robe, but realized it was near the front of the bed, too far to reach. She would have to turn and face Michelle, wearing only the articles of her shame.

She broke down, standing there, the day's unshed tears welling out of her eyes and rolling down her face without a sound. Just rolling, rolling down and in another moment she was going to sob—

"I just came to drop my books off. I'm going to see Ginny now." Michelle dropped her books with a clatter and left as quickly as she had promised.

The surprise stopped the tears. Michelle had seen—everything—yet she had not intruded. She had given Amanda the privacy she needed, had been—kind. Amanda tried to smile, but couldn't, and suddenly the tears came again, with racking sobs and her soaked face pressed hard to her pillow.

* * *

They were sitting at the dinner table, but neither one was eating.

"Do you think Amanda will come down?" asked Michelle.

"She'll come down—because she has to," answered Ginny. "I know."

"You mean—you . . . ?"

"My parents were mad at me last year—my grades were too low. I stole a copy of a test in advance." Ginny gave Michelle an odd little smile. "I was caught."

On the other side of Ginny, Sherry Paxton was all ears.

"Were you," Michelle paused, but her curiosity drove her on, "punished?"

"Yes, downstairs. With the cane."

"Why didn't you ever tell me? What was it like?"

"Look!"

Sherry's command was unnecessary. *Every* head turned to watch Amanda's entrance into the dining room.

Her face was very pale, making her lips look unnaturally red. Her eyes were huge and blue as she scanned the silent staring faces. She had nowhere to go.

"Amanda," Ginny called in a loud clear voice. Amanda looked at her, but Ginny was not at all certain that she understood. "Come sit with us," she continued, moving away from Michelle and gesturing to the space between them. This maneuver brought her next to Sherry.

"Move down," she hissed, and Sherry obeyed, hiding her resentment in her vast bulk. She wondered if some day she ought to do something very bad.

A flurry of whispers raced through the watching girls. Those of the upper class were enlightening the younger ones, who listened eagerly to the purple tales. They told of Ginny's previous sins, and painted lurid pictures of Amanda's coming sorrow.

And all the time they spoke, and listened, they watched, but it was not Amanda's face they saw. That single collective look when she entered had been enough. It had been frightening to see her pride's control stretched so gossamer thin—every fine line of her face exaggerated by the terrible tension of her emotions. The schoolgirls had seen all this at a glance, and felt their own guilt—for Amanda was one of them and they had turned on her. Still they could not look away entirely—with an awful prurient fascination their eyes were drawn down . . .

Cold, I'm so cold, thought Amanda.

They watched her legs, still now, sheathed in silk. The blackness each girl had hidden away was before their eyes.

Ginny saw that Amanda didn't hear her. She stood up, walked over to Amanda, and took her arm.

"Come sit with us,' she repeated, and Amanda came along, floating by her side, pale as a ghost.

"Do you want something to eat?"

"No, thank you."

"I can get you something if you want."

"No, thank you."

Ginny could think of nothing more to say to Amanda, who stared silently, as if trying to see beyond the dark horizon of her future.

Michelle quietly placed her hand on Amanda's wrist.

The dinner hour slowly passed: some girls ate, others did not—or could not. Their image of Amanda, constantly reinforced by furtive glances, slowly penetrated into their hearts.

Few would ever admit they loved her then.

"It's almost seven. I think I'll go now," said Ginny.

She touched Amanda's shoulder as she got up, then bent down and whispered in Michelle's ear, "Stay with her."

Michelle and Amanda went up to their room together.

Their old antagonism lay on the floor between them. A beginning friendship lacked words to express itself, while the clock ticked on.

They held hands, with only a small bedside light on, and finally began to talk of old days and the children they once were.

* * *

Miss Markham quickly buttoned her blouse in her locked office. She felt cold, and slipped her arms back into her white cashmere sweater. She crossed her arms, pulling the soft material over her breasts as she hugged herself, waiting for Amanda.

* * *

"When I was six years old, I used to walk down a clover path to a stream I liked. Once I stepped on a bee and ran all the way to the house screaming, 'I got hung, I got hung, I got hung!' "

"Stung," Michelle smiled, then the smile faded as she looked over Amanda's shoulder.

Amanda stayed facing Michelle, not turning her head.

"It's nine o'clock."

"Yes," said Amanda.

Michelle leaned forward and kissed Amanda lightly on the lips. Amanda was motionless, cold.

"I think you better go now."

"Yes."

Amanda stood up, looking down at her smaller roommate. At the last second before she turned to go out the door, she had a sudden desire to swing back and embrace Michelle, just hold to her desperately—but then she had turned another degree and the moment was gone.

She opened the door and stepped out into the corridor. She didn't look back or close the door. It was enough that she told her feet to keep moving.

Miss Markham came immediately to Amanda's knock. They did not speak—instead, the teacher simply took Amanda's arm, holding her with the firm grasp of one who knows her duty.

They walked through the silent school, stopping at the basement door. Miss Markham opened the door and ushered Amanda through. She closed the door behind them, while her pupil waited on the first step. She took Amanda's arm again, but now they were pressed close in the narrow stairwell. Amanda felt her teacher's softness, her warmth and she said, "We're sisters," but it was so soft that no one could hear her, just a whisper of breath as they took the last step and faced Madame Girard.

The Directrice sat behind a huge antique mahogany desk. Her face was in shadow, because of the lights behind her, but the desk was brightly illuminated. The cane was a diagonal yellow streak across the red brown polished wood.

About ten feet in front of the desk was a device that Amanda recognized as a converted gymnasium horse. The handles had been removed, and it had been recovered with black leather. Its height seemed to be just below that of Amanda's waist.

Miss Markham led Amanda close around the horse, holding her between it and Madame Girard.

The Directrice stood up behind her desk, her dark shadow reaching them. Amanda shuddered in her teacher's grasp, staring at the looming figure before the lights.

The first command came in a matter of fact tone, and caught Amanda off guard, for it ignored her completely.

"Frances"—this was the first time Amanda had heard her teacher addressed by her first name—"take off your sweater."

Miss Markham released Amanda's arm, took off her cashmere sweater and laid it on a corner of the desk. She stepped back to stand next to Amanda as before. There seemed to be something different about the way her teacher moved, but Amanda could not look further as her eyes were suddenly arrested by a tiny movement. Madame's hand had begun to move toward the cane. Amanda watched in fascination as the pale strong hand moved across the polished wood. The Directrice grasped the handle with her right hand and flipped the weapon up, catching it about the middle with her other hand. She held it straight across her chest.

Madame Girard spoke again to Miss Markham, but now her voice was harsh with the exercise of power.

"Lift up her skirt."

Amanda could do nothing as her teacher reached down and grasped her hem with both hands. In a second she was naked from the waist down, save for the fragile black silk that marked her.

The Directrice's eyes burned once over Amanda's lower body, ascertaining that her orders had been carried out.

"Turn around."

Amanda obeyed. She stood directly in front of the horse. Miss Markham was now to her right, still holding her skirt high.

Amanda could hear Madame Girard's footsteps, high heels clicking on the parquet floor. The Directrice stopped, unseen, behind Amanda and to the left.

Amanda's breath was shallow and rapid—her hands were soaked with sweat as they dug into the leather covering of the horse.

"Bend over."

Amanda's upper body formed a low hanging arc over the horse. Her offered buttocks were high now, straining against the thin silk that covered them.

"Take her panties down."

Miss Markham inserted her fingers on both sides of the fragile garment. With a sudden jerk, Amanda was divested of her last protection.

The cane whistled like a diving hawk. Amanda took the impact, and bore it for a second, and then the shock wave of pain burst through her nerves and she screamed and jerked her arms up—only to let them fall, and remain in position, her bare white ass bisected by a livid red streak.

"Frances, step around and hold Amanda's arms."

Amanda could not see her teacher's face, only the long delicate fingers coming to grasp her wrists. She tried to raise her head, but still she could only see the open V of Miss Markham's blouse, the deep cleavage—that was the difference she had noticed, the softness—

The whistling hawk struck again, scattering Amanda's thoughts as the cane burned into her flesh. She tried to move but couldn't, held by the hands she loved, she could only cry out, she was crying, blurred eyes closer to her sister, no bra that was the difference, soft breasts near her face and then the hawk again, the searing talon and she screamed and tried to raise her head, arcing her back and offering herself to the cane coming down again and again and again.

The voice came from far away. She heard it as though through a curtain of fire and water.

"Stand up, Amanda."

40

Someone nice helped her up. Her skirt fell down—the sudden abrasion on her mistreated skin tore a gasp out of her.

"Pull up your panties."

Amanda reached down and pulled them up, slowly, mechanically, as her vision cleared through the rain of tears. Her hands passed over the burning welts, the silk desperately tight over the swollen flesh, and suddenly she just wanted to squeeze herself, grab her behind and rub the pain away—but she didn't dare.

She freed her hands and turned to face Madame Girard; tremulous, but with honor.

"Amanda, I believe you have learned your lesson. You can not go on as you have. Do you understand?"

"Yes."

"Tell Miss Markham that you are sorry for the trouble you have caused."

"Miss Markham, I"—her voice broke for a second as the pain went through her and then she caught it, she would not fail now before her teacher—"I am sorry. I will not cause trouble for you in the future."

"You may go back to your room now, Amanda."

Amanda was still looking at Miss Markham.

Would her teacher go with her?

The soft brown eyes said no.

Amanda turned and walked alone toward the stairs.

With each upward step the welts gave off another burst of fire. Her loins were enveloped with heat, and her hands shuddered with the effort of keeping them at their sides.

Time expanded, and her mind played tricks. It seemed to take forever to reach the top—at the same time her thoughts floated through the door, wandered off with Raymond past a shadow of a church—she turned the knob. The door was heavy, and the sudden effort of shoving it open brought fresh tears to her eyes as her legs simply gave way.

Amanda watched, as if from far away, as her knees buckled in slow motion just as she had imagined hours before in Madame Girard's office. She came to rest kneeling on the top step as the door swung back and shut with a loud click. Amanda rested her head against it, and reached back with both hands to sooth her soft wounded flesh.

At first Amanda thought the sound was inside her own head, but then she realized it had come up through the wood from the basement. She remembered an experiment she had done as a child: resting her head on a table, she had reached around to the other side and lightly scratched it. She remembered the peculiar amplification of the sound waves traveling through wood—when she had raised her head, the scratching was inaudible.

Now she was hearing high heeled shoes on the parquet floor. A word—indistinct—the sense of a large cat, purring with barely sheathed claws.

They thought she was gone.

They had heard the door open and shut.

Suddenly Amanda had to see.

She turned 180 degrees, crawled down two steps with silent hands, and peered over the edge of the staircase.

Madame Girard still held the cane. Miss Markham was on her knees before the Directrice, forehead touching the floor in an attitude of penance. Madame stepped forward like a dancer, her skirt swirling above her knees for a second, and then she was astride the kneeling teacher. The dark brown dress hid Miss Markham's upper body from view.

The cane extended like the wand of an Indian snake charmer. Slowly Frances's head began to rise under the folds of the dress. She stopped at the juncture of the parted thighs.

Madame place her left hand over the diffuse outline of hair beneath the cloth. Her hand tightened, urging the kneeling woman's face forward. The cane was poised over the bent buttocks, still hidden by a plaid skirt.

The Directrice spoke. "Now," she said, and in the same moment the cane descended with a sharp, authoritive smack.

Amanda felt a reciprocal quiver in her own behind—she reached back with one hand to hold herself as she watched the Directrice relaxing in pleasure, swaying slightly to the soft hidden tongue.

Amanda felt the heat under her hand, had to get closer to it, and now her hand was under her skirt, under the tight panties, squeezing urgently as she watched the scene below. Her breath was louder and louder in her own ears, and she knew she had to move her hand around.

I can't stay. The thought broke across her consciousness like a revelation. She rose to her feet in one quick silent motion, both hands free now to handle the heavy door. She moved it with the same burst of adrenalin—she shut it behind her with the care of a safecracker.

She was alone, in the deserted first floor hallway of Madame Girard's Academy.

* * *

Michelle rarely made it past ten. She would pick up her hairbrush and say, very solemnly, "Tonight I am going to brush my hair one hundred strokes." Then her hair would fly in every direction, she'd make a face in the mirror, laugh and toss the hairbrush on the bureau.

She had the brush in her hand now—she tried a stroke and thought of her roommate. Amanda, now: one hundred strokes, regular as clockwork. Placid—like a cow she is—that's how I used to think of her.

But now I've seen her cut to the quick—I'll not forget her face when she entered the dining room—it haunts me even now—forget this hairbrush—I can't stop thinking of her for a minute, especially with her downstairs, bent over now more than likely—poor American girl.

Suddenly Michelle thought of the childhood stories they had told each other this evening, and the rush of tenderness with no outlet brought her to her feet. She looked at her gamine face in the mirror and said, "This is for you, Amanda," and kissed the reflection of her lips.

The mirror gave no more response than Amanda had earlier. Michelle threw the hairbrush across the room.

I hope they—and then she thought again of Amanda's hand in hers ("I got hung, I got hung, I got hung").

Michelle smiled.

I hope they do not hurt you too much. I hope your man is worth it.

Michelle had never believed the gossip about Amanda and Miss Markham.

She was a wise child who had lived through a succession of "aunts" since her mother had died as a journalist in Vietnam. Sometimes there had been two "aunts" at once—for a month or more all living together in that big dark Irish house.

Michelle had learned—too much perhaps. Some-

44

times she wondered if that was why her father had sent her away.

Michelle walked over and picked up the hairbrush.

It's no different here, she thought, and she would have thrown the brush back the other way had not Amanda opened the door.

Michelle laid the brush on the bureau in one quick motion, stepped across the room, and took Amanda's hands in both of hers. It was like a dance. Michelle gently swung the taller girl around until they had exchanged positions. Then she disengaged one hand, reached back, and closed the door with a decisive shove.

They stared into each other's eyes. Amanda took a step closer as their hands strained together; they were inches away from a kiss when Michelle saw the repressed shudder, the flicker of Amanda's eyes as the pain shot through her.

Michelle stopped.

"Amanda," she said, "lie down on the bed."

Amanda started to protest, but then accepted the command gratefully. She turned, slipped out of her high heels, and lay face down on her bed.

Michelle brought the cold cream over and laid it on the bed by Amanda's side.

She stroked Amanda's hair lightly.

"I'll get your skirt off, love. Just raise up a little."

The skirt was tossed on the bureau. Michelle knelt over the prone girl's thighs. This time Amanda raised her hips without being asked. Michelle's gentle fingers slid under the silk. Delicately, she raised the tight panties above the scored flesh. Then she began to draw them down.

"Michelle."

"Yes?" The Irish girl stopped her motion, fingers

just a fraction of an inch above Amanda's skin, so close that she could feel the heat rising from the punished backside.

"Tell me . . ." Amanda turned her head to one side and looked at Michelle—held the awkward position for a second, and then buried her face in the pillow again.

Michelle waited, hands almost beginning to tremble—

"Tell me . . ." Amanda raised her head again, then, unable to speak, she arched her back still more, the motion forcing Michelle's fingers against her.

Amanda gave a little cry, and then she got the words out. "Tell me what my bottom looks like."

In one motion Michelle jerked Amanda's panties to her knees. She hiked up her own skirt, so that her stockinged legs pressed close to Amanda's as she crouched above her. Very deliberately, she set her hands on the bare unmarked whiteness of Amanda's upper thighs.

"Do you want the cream first?" she asked, fingers squeezing into the vulnerable flesh of the girl beneath her.

"No, please, tell me . . ."

And then Amanda arched her back again, raising her buttocks as if begging . . .

Michelle felt a wild joy inflame her, a heat that devoured her breath as she began to speak.

"The blood has come up." Her breath came harshly after each short sentence. "All your bottom is pink and red. Every stripe is a raised welt. They're *so* dark red"—now her fingers were following her vice—"and this one"—she ran her index finger across the unbearably tender skin—"is almost black, for here"—she ran her finger back again, as

46

Amanda shuddered—"she hit you in the same place—twice."

Amanda gave a cry like a cat outside in the rain, and then Michelle filled both hands with cold cream and pressed them hard into the burning flesh. She squeezed and massaged, squeezed and massaged, and maybe she was doing to too hard, but she couldn't stop, anyway Amanda was pushing back against her, loving the coolness and crying beneath her hands.

After a time they slowed down; Amanda's tears dried against the pillow. Michelle got more cold cream for her hands and rubbed it in gently, tenderly.

Amanda's body rocked leisurely with her friend's caressing motions. The secret place between her thighs rubbed against the bed—involuntarily she started to spread her legs but came up against the barrier of her own panties, and Michelle's thighs.

I could stop now, and thank Michelle, thought Amanda, but I'm floating in a dream world and I do not choose to stop—I'm just a lazy, dreamy girl floating on the waves . . .

Amanda rolled over on her back.

There was a flash of pain, but it seemed far away, like heat lightning outside a darkened window.

Amanda smiled at Michelle; she looked into her friend's eyes, and told her in that dreamy voice, "Take my panties all the way off."

Then when Michelle was at her feet, all bonds lifted, Amanda slowly spread her long legs.

She beckoned the Irish girl closer, and took her face between both her hands.

Amanda knew her friend was willing, knew that she had only to press down—but she wanted to prolong the moment. She enjoyed the sudden knowledge of her control, and she ran her fingers through Michelle's wild red curls.

"You didn't get past ten tonight, did you?"

"No." Michelle looked straight into Amanda's blue eyes. "I was thinking of you."

"Were you?"

"Yes."

Amanda's hand tightened. "Show me," she said, and then she pressed down hard until she felt the kiss of love between her thighs.

* * *

Raymond drifted the big car to a stop thirty feet from the locked iron gates. He took his shoes and socks off, left the keys in the ignition, and checked his pockets to make sure he still had the carrots.

No thieves in this neighborhood, he said to himself, and then without consciously thinking of her his heart suddenly skipped a beat and he said "Amanda," the sound only in his head and now as he climbed the wall he said "Amanda," no sound just a breath before he jumped, "Amanda," and as he walked, the air warm but the grass cold against his feet, "Amanda," calling her name with every silent breath.

* * *

Amanda heard her name gently reverberating in her head as she slept naked in Michelle's arms. Suddenly she was wide awake.

"Amanda."

She heard it, not as a sound, but as a vibration in her own head.

"Amanda."

It came with the rhythm of breathing. She didn't bother to check the clock. It was time.

Amanda tried to roll away quietly and get up, but Michelle just moaned sleepily and held her tighter. Amanda tried to roll the other way and the same thing happened.

Amanda had to smile at the ridiculous situation. She turned her head to look at Michelle. A shaft of moonlight came through a gap in the curtains and illuminated the Irish girl's face. Amanda wondered how she could ever have thought that Michelle had sharp features. She had a dear face, relaxed with sleep and love, and Amanda kissed her very lightly on the forehead and said, "Michelle, darling, loosen your arms so I can get up now."

Like a girl obeying a hypnotist Michelle's hands let go, and Amanda rolled free. She watched, smiling, as her friend settled back into sleep, arms now hugging her own body.

"Amanda."

The sound came again deep in her brain, and suddenly she felt very naked standing there, as though Raymond could see her. She moved to her closet and took out a fresh white blouse.

* * *

Raymond slid back the dead bolt on the stable door and tried to open it, but there was resistance at the bottom. He reached down and turned the wood block there, and then the door gave and he was out of the moonlight and into the darkness of the stable.

Ears went back on giant heads as the horses registered his presence, but none of them whinnied or

49

kicked because as soon as the door opened Raymond had started talking in a low confiding monotone.

"Hello my friends, how are my beauties, what's this my son, I'm Attila the Hun, come for a midnight ride across the steppes, oh it's three o'clock, sorry horses, where's Ginger, there you are you beautiful palomino, yes I see why you're Amanda's favorite, yes I love you too but don't take the finger with the carrot, no, take it easy, let me snap this rope on, that's a good girl, have another piece, good for the eyes, yes you like carrots, yes . . ." He kept talking quietly as he led her out of the stable, closed the door behind him, and locked it with two deft motions.

'Always leave a door just the way you found it.' That had been his father's cardinal rule. Raymond's parents had been small farmers who discovered they had no empathy for plants. Nothing would grow right for them. Animals were a different story. If you didn't know what to do with your pet, if you were driving south and couldn't pack the horses, let the Navarres have them for a while.

Finally Hernando Navarre got smart. He fenced in the ten acre pasture (fenced in the weeds and thistles and misshapen trees), stuck chicken wire up for dog runs, put cages in the loft for cats, and the Navarre Animal Boarding Home came into existence. Raymond grew up with every kind of beast around: always several horses (their rich owners basking in Bermuda), always several dogs (their rich owners basking in Miami), always cats, sometimes mice, once a snake.

A carelessly opened door could have had serious consequences with such a menagerie; Raymond was always careful, and he had never lost the habit.

As a child, he had made a point of riding at least

once every strange horse that came to their farm—
now he put one hand on Ginger's mane and leaped
lightly on to her back. Amanda had said that the
bridles and saddles were locked up, but he had told
her that all he needed was a rope.

He wrapped his thighs around the horse's warm
back and watched her powerful shoulder muscles
move as she started to walk. All his concentration
was on the horse now, as he explained just what they
were going to do.

"Ginger we're going to walk right next to that big
building—no we're not going to the paddock—no
we're going this way, I know you've never gone this
way before, there you go, good girl, you know
Amanda, oh Jesus Amanda, now don't put your ears
back Ginger, I love you too, well we're going to pre-
tend you're a circus horse, yes that's it, the first
window on this side, the second floor, good girl now
stay perfectly still, perfectly still, I'm going to stand
on your back . . ."

* * *

The blouse was no trouble, she slipped it over her
shoulders not bothering with a bra; she felt a quiver
through her body as the fine material rubbed over
her nipples. She grabbed a skirt next—there was no
time for underwear, she didn't want any underwear—and without thinking pulled it on.

"Ouch!" She couldn't restrain the sudden cry at
the abrasion of the fabric over her bruised behind.
She stopped, hands on her hips, and looked at Michelle, whose eyes opened in the moonlight.

"Where have you gone Amanda?"

Very carefully she pulled the skirt the rest of the
way and cautiously fastened it.

"Are you going to him now?" Again the voice from the bed.

"Amanda."

Raymond's voice was terribly loud in her head.

"Yes, I'm going."

She meant I'm coming, I'm coming to you Raymond.

She moved toward the window, not seeing the pain in Michelle's eyes.

"I'll help you, love."

That's all I can do, thought Michelle. That's all I can do.

Raymond stood on Ginger's back, but even with his arms raised he was two feet below the window. For the first time he made his whispered breath into a true sound.

"Amanda."

She drew the curtains wide and looked down into the face of the man she loved.

Michelle was getting up. "Let me put my nightgown on."

"Amanda." He smiled up at her as his bare feet sent messages through Ginger's warm back—be still, be still, be still . . .

The window rose, stuck, then rose higher, a girl pushing at either end.

"I forgot my shoes."

"Do you want your boots?"

"No, the heels."

(The ones I held while he kissed me, the ones I put on while he held me)

"Get your foot over—now the other one, I've got your arms." Michelle wanted to kiss Amanda good-bye but suddenly she was below as her weight buckled Raymond's knees and he let his feet slide down the flanks of the horse.

Then she was a white blur on the horse looking gray in the moonlight, then she vanished, then Michelle saw them again, clear of the tree that had momentarily blocked her vision.

Suddenly Amanda seemed to rise, he was holding her, he was dark in the night only his hands showed white as he lifted her, the dark skirt high, and Michelle never heard Amanda's scream as he entered her for in that last second he covered her lips with his, but she felt the stab of pain as if in her own body, and then the rhythm of the man, of the horse, and Michelle watched until they disappeared into the night, tears streaming down her face.

* * *

He opened the door quietly and laid her down on the front seat; she seemed weightless, boneless, soft rippling water.

"Wait for me here, darling. I must take Ginger back."

Amanda looked up at him and said, "Yes." Her eyes were shining in the night.

She curled up on the seat and laid her head behind the wheel, where he would sit, and let the world spin over her.

* * *

She heard the door, then his hand was under her head; she raised up enough to let him get in, then snuggled close and laid her head in his lap.

The motor caught, startling her a little, and she put out a hand and stroked his thigh.

"What happened to your motorcycle?"

"It wasn't mine. I borrowed it from a friend that

53

day, just to go out for a spin." Raymond smiled down at her, caressing her cheek with a teasing finger. "What if I hadn't taken that ride? You might still be a virgin now."

Amanda smiled back at him with complete confidence. "You would have found me," she said, "somehow."

* * *

Captain Beasley's letter never reached Amanda—but a week later he did get a postcard from her. There was a New York address; the note was very short. She told him that she had a part in an Off Broadway play.

Part II

Yankee Doodle
(Raymond's story)

The girls were beautiful playing in the sea. I sat on the beach at Ocean City, watching them duck through the waves, splashing each other, then turning in mock apprehension, holding hands, while a big one crashed harmlessly against their backs. Now and then I could catch a flutter of conversation above the noises of surf, gulls, and radios, but I didn't need words to know their happiness. Amanda, my wife, and Lisa, my lover—they played like children, cares left on the shore. Watching my beautiful loves I imagined delights planned for the morrow, and I would have been completely happy if I had just seen Amanda laugh. Yet I knew the smile she was wearing was the closest she could come. In the seven years of our marriage, I had never seen Amanda laugh.

Amanda's father killed himself after she ran away with me. Not right away, you understand—first he came up to New York to "bring her home." He caught up with us one night in the little Greenwich Village theater where we were rehearsing my play, The Bass Place. Amanda was sitting before a blue painted stream, dangling a fake hooked fishing line into the non-existent water. She was playing a country girl who had retreated from her suitors to try to catch a giant and wily largemouth bass. Her father came in, and called her in his commanding, naval officer's voice—but she didn't break character. She told him to keep his voice down, for he was disturbing the fish.

Captain Beasley came up and took her by the arm. There wasn't really a scene—Amanda was calm but immovable. I watched the short struggle. Amanda looked at me once and then back at her father. "My home is with Raymond now," she said.

Her father left then, without another word.

We found out later he drove straight through to his office at Norfolk—it only took him seven hours, so he must have kept the car at eighty the whole way. The Navy records that he reached his office at three in the morning—he had to sign in with a guard to get inside. He locked himself in, and unlocked his desk, where he kept his service issue .45 automatic. He put the barrel of the gun in his mouth, and blasted the back of his head onto the wall behind him.

There was no note.

The Captain hadn't bothered with a will either. Amanda still being seventeen at this time, all of the Beasley fortune went to his widow, Sandy. She cashed it in and left for Europe before Amanda was eighteen.

We never saw a cent of the money that had surrounded Amanda when she was growing up.

In the space of a year Amanda lost her father, her mother disappeared, and her inheritance vanished.

Amanda took it well.

In fact, she hardly showed any emotion at all—which killed my play. The show went on, but only to make a grand, one night flop.

The one critic who came was merciless about Amanda's wooden performance, but it was wasted venom, for she didn't read the review.

I was glad the play was finished; it was agony to see Amanda try to get up and say her lines with any kind of verve; and the more we had rehearsed the more I realized that the play simply wasn't that good. I didn't blame Amanda in the slightest—I only came to love her more with each passing day.

We got married on her eighteenth birthday. Benjamin Hillery, my ex-producer, didn't want to know me any more—so I borrowed the money for the fee from a chess tournament director I knew (it was my chess that had kept us alive through the months after Captain Beasley's suicide—it was chess, not playwriting, that I now knew would be my future). A justice of the peace did the honors in a dirty graffiti scarred government building in downtown Manhattan. The black couple behind us were the witnesses—we waited, and witnessed for them in turn.

For a honeymoon Amanda and I took the Path train into New Jersey. I spent the last of our money on a cheap motel (we could no longer afford New York prices) and then I took her to bed. Amanda gave herself with an almost frightening abandon.

In the morning she placidly came along with me to the edge of the highway. We had used the subway to get around in the city, so I had sold my car to pay bills. Now, having no alternative, I stuck out my thumb, and we waited for a ride.

* * *

We settled in Easton, Pennsylvania. I considered this a reasonable spot since this small town was located roughly halfway between New York and Philadelphia—so I could play in chess tournaments in either direction.

Amanda didn't care where we lived.

* * *

The next three years were occupied by the struggle to survive. I worked at any odd job, while studying chess fanatically. Amanda, who had never touched a dish except to eat off it, became an expert waitress.

One day I asked her why she never laughed, and my life changed. "How can I laugh when my head hurts?" Amanda snapped.

"How long have you been having headaches?" I asked.

"Since the day—" she faltered, and then went on—"since the day my father died."

"Why didn't you tell me?"

"I took Bufferin," she said. "There was no need to tell you. You have enough to do."

I took her in my arms, but all my muscles were tight with rage. "You tell me. Anything like this, you tell me. And we're going to get rid of those headaches." I wanted to kill someone, but the man to blame was already dead.

It was only much later that I was able to forgive Captain Beasley for the damage his death had caused his daughter; after we had our first son I realized how it was possible to love a child too much.

But that son was still five years away in this sum-

mer of 1973—right then we had pain to contend
with.

Amanda went to a doctor, and then a therapist;
money was no object as far as her pain was concerned (my parents were never well off, and they
were getting a little old for animals now—still, they
had more than we did, and they helped when they
learned of the problem, for they loved Amanda as I
did.

There was nothing physically wrong; just a psychic
guilt like a knife in her skull. The therapist, an ear-
nest youthful fellow (older than Amanda but younger
than me) told Amanda that she wasn't to blame for
her father's death. His death was his choice. She
must now put that behind her and live her own life.

It was simple advice, something I could have told
her—but she needed to hear it from someone else.
The headaches stopped; Amanda declared herself
cured and ended her therapy; but still she didn't
laugh.

*   *   *

The year that I learned about the headaches was
also the year that I became a master of chess. The
year after that, I met Lisa. Today, watching Lisa and
Amanda together, seeing their obvious happiness, I
wondered if Lisa might be the one who could take
my wife's hand and lead Amanda past the shadow of
death to the joyous laughter of life—but then I realized there was no use. I had tried for years now
without making the slightest impression (and Richard
Pryor, George Carlin, and Steve Martin were no
help either). To laugh without restraint is to lose
control—and Amanda only lost control in bed. That

happiness, joyous though it may be, is not the type that easily translates to belly laughs.

So I willed myself to forget about laughter; I knew it could never be forced; I let my eyes focus on one who always had a laugh for me—I looked at Lisa, bouncing through the waves in her red bikini, chattering all the while.

And yet I couldn't really focus on her, for nothing is simple in this world. Seeing Lisa in public was always a form of double vision for me. There was the bright and laughing chatterbox—and there was the darker, yet more beautiful vision of her silent and nude.

I lay back on the towel, in the slight coolness of shade beneath the beach umbrella, and thought of how I had met Lisa for the first time.

* * *

From the age of fourteen and onward for many years, I hated nuns. It was Lisa who changed me. Now this hatred did not have a conventional source. I didn't have bad experiences in some strict Catholic high school, nor did my parents force any dogmatic religious impressions on me. For that matter, despite my Spanish name, I'm not even a Catholic!

My father fell in love with a gentle Pennsylvania girl, a member of the Society of Friends (better known as Quakers) and he changed his religion to please her (perhaps another way to put it is that she became his religion). So I was born a member of the Society of Friends, and my parents took me to Meeting regularly once a year on Christmas (one might say that by the time I was born my mother's religion had become my father—formal piety was never important to either of them). I have always been grateful to the Friends for quite possibly saving my life—their pacifistic ideals (which I must admit I don't share) gave me, as a lifelong member, a legal Conscientious Objector status which kept me out of the Vietnam War.

The reason I hated nuns was because I was a hitchhiker. I grew up in a rural village five miles from the nearest bookstore. If one didn't have a car, the only way to get around was to hitchhike. Frequently I saw nuns pass me by on the highway, always four at a time inside a big new American car. There was plenty of room for an additional passenger in the back, but defying all I had ever heard of Christian charity, they never stopped. I was out there in all sorts of climactic conditions, but the sight of a soaked hitchhiker never moved the good Sisters of Hypocrisy—perhaps they thought I would mess up the upholstery.

The worst incident of this type occurred just before my first meeting with Lisa. It was a Friday night in January, and I was on my way to a weekend chess tournament in Binghamton, New York. I had left Amanda with a kiss at about 5:00 P.M.—after finishing my day's work at my latest Manpower assignment. I had spent the usual horrible day loading a tractor trailer with 100 lb. sacks of chicken feed— it was eleven o'clock now, I was tired, and it was snowing. Rides were sparse, and I was wet, cold, and shivering when I got off at the last exit in Binghamton, a little country roadway called route 47B. It was about five miles of fairly desolate countryside before I would get to the dilapidated motel where the tournament was to be held. I'd played there before. It wasn't the Waldorf, but it was cheap, and that is the only criteria that matters to a chess organizer— in this case, a sweet little man named Ron Filken.

61

There are a few courageous souls like him who bring chess to the wilderness—but there has never been any money in that racket.

Anyway, the last time I had played there, I had managed to get a ride from the exit right to the motel. Few cars took 47B, but those that did generally went at least that far, as the only thing between the highway and the motel was worn down farmland.

The snow was beating on my face as I started walking down the exit. Suddenly I saw yellow headlights catching the falling snow. Immediately I spun around, square to the road, my arm extended straight out almost blocking the path of the oncoming car, my bare thumb (I had shucked my right glove as I spun, because I knew from experience that a barehanded signal increased the percentage of rides) stabbing upward at the snowflakes, rigid.

The car slowed down—it was only going about five miles per hour as it approached me—and I slipped my duffel bag off my shoulder in preparation for throwing it inside. I relaxed a little, because I was sure that this car would take me all the way to the motel—and a fortunate thing that was, as it was the only car on the road. The general rule was that only people who had hitchhiked themselves would pick up hitchhikers, but occasionally weather like this could bring out compassion in people from whom you would never expect it. I wondered who was driving—and then my entire body went tense as I saw black and white framing around women's faces. Nuns! Yet I couldn't believe they wouldn't stop. I had never had a car that approached so slowly and didn't stop, but even as they closed the gap an awful thought began to seize me: nuns are extremely cautious drivers, and it was possible that they were just slowing down for the curve of the exit, which had quite a bit more snow on it than the highway. They weren't intending to stop for me at all! I knew it in my heart before they got to me, but I didn't believe it until the right rear bumper slowly slid by. Then I started to run—an awkward procedure since I was holding my duffel bag plus one glove with my left hand, and I lurched all over the place in the fresh snow. I could not run quite as fast as the car. The nuns didn't speed up—they just kept a few sadistic feet in front of me and watched in their rear view mirror until I faltered and gave up.

I watched their taillights disappear into the snowstorm, and I found myself in blackness, on a country road devoid of streetlights. I had heard my chess set rattling as I ran, and I hoped that none of my pieces were broken. I put my duffel bag back over my shoulder, put my right glove on, and started walking. It took me more than two hours to get to the motel. I didn't see another car.

* * *

After the first time we made love, I discovered that Lisa knew almost nothing about sex, or her own body. The only position she'd tried was missionary, and the closest she'd been to pornography was Erica Jong's *Fear of Flying* (or to put it another way, she thought that work of literature was pornography!). When I swived her she was open, loose, and extravagantly wet with her forbidden excitement. I loved the last part but of course the looseness gave me little physical pleasure. It surprised me that she didn't have a clue about how to use her own inner muscles—didn't even know (in 1977!) that she had them. I was astonished by her ignorance—but then again, I loved teaching her.

One day in a hotel room I made her lie naked across my lap as I sat up fully dressed on the bed. Her feet were to my left, and I had her spread her legs a little as I put the longest finger of my left hand into her cunt. She was wet as ever. I told her to squeeze my finger, and I told her what to do to make her inner muscles work. Nothing happened, and I spanked her small, soft behind—not too hard—with my right hand. She tried again without success, and I spanked her again, a little harder.

It was after the third time that I felt it, though felt is almost too strong a word. It was like hearing the faintest touch of a whisper delicately wrapping itself about my finger. This time my right hand *caressed* her ass—and then I made her squeeze me again. I alternated rewards and punishments until finally, gasping, her bottom glowing pink, she came around my finger that was grasped tightly in the midst of her secrets.

That was five months ago. It was three years before that that I met Lisa—how could I have imagined such a scene then? I came out of the snow into the motel, and I saw Lisa (though of course I didn't know her name then) sitting around a chessboard with two other girls and a young man. They looked up as I came in, and my gaze quickly zeroed in on one of the other girls. Ah, there's the pretty one, I said to myself—and I gave her a quick vague smile as I turned to the desk to check in.

I'm always ashamed to recall that first dismissive glance. All I saw, on my way to the face of the conventionally pretty girl, was a top-heavy woman with a plain face, undistinguished brown hair, and dowdy clothes—not much of a description to be sure, but enough to set her outside the plane of my desire.

But then again, I had not yet heard her speak, or

seen her smile. I would be touched by both in the next few minutes, and almost immediately my tune began to change.

* * *

I looked across the water and saw Lisa and Amanda, momentarily out of breath, leaning against each other in thigh high water. The gentle surf jogged their legs a little, and I saw a little curl go by that must have pulled the sand from beneath their feet. They spun around sideways, clutching each other—Lisa was laughing.

They looked over at me and waved, and I waved back, wondering what they saw—a man sitting none too comfortably on a beach towel, well tanned but ill at ease—I have never truly enjoyed the heated communal pleasures of the beach.

Sometimes I get confused with all the different roles I have to play—but most of the time I enjoy the bizarre contrasts.

For example, back at the Binghamton Center Inn (far right wing was more like it!) a typical transformation occurred: I walked up to the desk clerk (and owner and manager, for that matter) and gave him a somewhat better smile than I had given the pretty girl—I was starting to thaw out.

"Hi, I'd like a single room for one night."

"Are you playing in the chess tournament?"

"Yes." I never elaborated when asked that sort of question, mainly because I thought that people should know who I was without me having to tell them. After all, I was a master now!

"Wouldn't you like it for two nights?" This was a logical question, as the tournament would take place over Saturday and Sunday, and it was now Friday night—or more precisely, 1:15 A.M. Saturday morning.

"Let's just make it one night for now," I said.

The man was used to the eccentricities of chess players. He gave a little shrug and passed the registration card over to me.

Of course, one man's eccentricity is another man's necessity. I used to go to such tournaments blind, even in winter—I'd get there with no place to stay at all. By 1974, when this Binghamton Winter Open took place, I had a little more ready cash. I would bring enough for one night in the motel (this saved me from looking for open churches on cold nights) and then after the tournament started it was easy for me to find a fellow chessplayer who was eager to give a master shelter for the night. In return I would explain the other player's mistakes, and suggest methods of improvement. Usually I would also play a number of offhand games with my benefactor (five minutes on the clock for each side) taking care to win them all. A master was a sort of otherworldly being to the average player—it would never do to break the illusion and let him know you were only human.

I paid for my room and walked over to the small group in the lobby. As I approached, the plain woman I had scarcely noticed smiled at me and asked, "Are you Raymond Navarre?"

It was a light, pleasant voice, with just the right touch of awe in it, yet underneath I could detect a faint edge of mockery. I smiled as I noticed that edge, and I thought to myself, yes, this girl has met some masters before—she's known some who really believe that the ability to foresee a ten move combination makes them divine.

I liked her immediately, and I tailored my answer

to please her. "Yes I am. I assume you're playing in the tournament."

Now this may seem a nothing opening line, but one must understand the strict hierarchy of the chess world. At the very pinnacle are the Grandmasters (whose titles are awarded for life!), then the International Masters, followed by your basic master, of whom I was one (and at that time there were only about a hundred in the whole country). Below the masters struggle the great mass of ordinary players, each specifically ranked by his U.S. Chess Federation rating. The most common conversational gambit in the chess world is "What's your rating?" In this way one quickly discovers whether your new acquaintance is superior or inferior.

Of course, these rankings apply only to players— almost beneath consideration lies the rest of the world: all those who do not play tournament chess. Sad to say, almost all women fit into this category. Every woman player I know has been hurt or humiliated by the question, "Who are you with?" The questioner, who often uses this as his brusque opening line, assumes (1) that the woman is not a player, and (2) that she could not have come to the tournament on her own; she must have a male escort.

So my spoken assumption was an unexpected gesture of respect, especially surprising from a master.

She smiled widely enough for a toothpaste ad, but started talking before the strain got to be too much.

"We all are. I'm Lisa Thatcher, and these are my students, the Spirit Lake High chess team!"

She introduced me to Paula, Stacy (the pretty one), and Peter, who put his arm around Stacy as he smiled at me.

"I helped Ron organize this tournament so that our team could get a free entry. Of course the school couldn't afford a dime for a chess road trip—they had already spent thousands on the football team! Anyway, when I learned you were coming tonight, we all agreed that we wouldn't be able to sleep until we knew you had arrived."

She was teasing me, of course. The mocking edge, the satire in her voice was clear. Yet her smile was genuine. I had no doubt that the main reason she was up had to do with her students. Wide awake at the prospect of a weekend far from parental supervision, they were probably poised to run amuck should Lisa retire early. A crucial point here is that at this time the drinking age in New York was eighteen—Spirit Lake is in Pennsylvania, where the minimum age is twenty-one. Peter looked eighteen to me—no doubt his teacher wanted to make sure he didn't make a beer run!

On the other hand, she *had* chosen to wait here, with a chessboard set up; and she knew my name. I didn't know how much of her admiration was real—but it existed, and that was enough for me. As I looked at her smile, I felt the completion of my metamorphosis. Two hours ago, I had been a freezing vagrant begging for a ride. Now I was truly (just as it says on the personal cards that I hand out to every pretty girl I meet) Raymond Navarre, Master of Chess.

"I see," I answered, with a perfect arrogance that took no account of her mockery. I looked straight into Lisa's eyes, watercolor swashes of blue—for a moment I saw something lost and yearning there, and then she laughed.

"I don't know why I should care so much. After all, it's just a game."

This stung me. If there's one thing I hate, it's hearing chess referred to as "just a game". I looked hard at Lisa and saw her laughing still, enjoying my discomfort. I forced a smile and said, "I'll show you a game."

I pulled up a chair and sat behind the black pieces.

"This is from my last tournament," I said, speaking generally to the whole group. "This guy, a high expert, thought he could draw with me by playing the Exchange French." I made a few quick moves. "Then suddenly he changes his mind and decides he can snatch two pawns!" I made a derisive snort and then continued to move the pieces, commenting on the strategies of both sides.

Peter occasionally asked a simple question, and Lisa came in with a few asides, but when I got to the rook sacrifice everyone became silent. Slowly they began to appreciate the depth of the combination, and they sat there, eyes fixed on the board, afraid even to look up at my face.

In this dilapidated motel, in the middle of this winter's night, they were seeing beauty of a sort they could only dream of—and never create.

The quiet move at the end took their breath away—the second rook casually coming over after five successive checks—and they sat there stunned while I explained that there was no way for White to avoid mate in four.

We all got up at the same time to say our good nights. There was no game playing between Lisa and me now, just a straightforward awareness of our interest. I took Lisa's hand and held it about two seconds longer than necessary.

"Thank you for showing us your game," she said.

"I'm glad you liked it," I replied. "Would you like me to put your set away?"

"Yes, thank you," she answered. As I started to

put the pieces in her bag, I heard her say to her students, "It's time to get some sleep. Don't leave any of your stuff down here."

"Mrs. Thatcher, when should we get up tomorrow?" It was Paula asking the question, in a small voice.

"The round is at ten, so use your own judgement. Remember, I'll be helping Ron in the morning, so you'll be on your own for breakfast."

I handed Lisa the bag and she accepted it with a nod of thanks. I watched as they walked away, and I thought, well she's married—perhaps I ought to be formal.

"Mrs. Thatcher," I called.

She turned immediately with that big smile. "I don't think I've seen you in any of my classes. You can call me Lisa."

"OK Lisa—good luck tomorrow!"

"Unless I play you, right?"

I smiled and she turned away, but I mumbled to myself, "Even then, perhaps even then."

I went up to my single room and unpacked nothing but my chess set. I set the pieces up carefully and gave a sigh of relief when I saw that none were broken.

Later I lay quietly in the darkness, feeling the slight soreness in my muscles from loading the truck. I thought of Lisa, of her sort of square upper body—or was that just her badly cut jacket? I thought of her smallish ass, but I couldn't imagine her legs, well hidden beneath her corduroys. She wore odd shoes for midwinter, cork soled clogs, heavily scuffed and coming apart at the toe. Nothing in her costume was designed to allure—even the colors where a mixture of muddy browns and grays—and nothing showed even a hint of fashion sense. Yet still I was fascinated, for I kept coming back to her face and the bright sunlight of her smile; I kept hearing the challenging edge in her cherry voice. Perhaps she should lose ten pounds and have a complete beauty makeover—but then I didn't really care. What mattered was that sudden softness in her eyes, some sadness hidden under the bright surface chaffing. I wanted to take her in my arms and have her snuggle against me—O I wanted to hold her.

It's true that love is stronger than hate. Had I not met Lisa, I might have spent the night contorted by rage against the nuns, strung tight by plans of revenge. But now they were almost forgotten. It's funny, but much later I learned that Lisa had gone to Catholic schools as a child. The Sisters were the first people she truly admired—for a long time she wanted to join their life of selflessness and contemplation. Finally the blossoming of her body took her down a different path, but I think that sometimes she still regretted her decision. Even when telling me of some Sister's foibles, or outright errors, she still spoke with a certain reverence. So I never told Lisa about my run through the snow, and I let my own anger fade away through neglect.

I did realize that first night that Lisa had a story of her own to tell me—but she was all bright and cheerful on the morrow, and it wasn't until three years later, after we had become lovers, that she chose to tell it to me.

A week before we met, that bright and laughing girl had almost committed suicide.

* * *

Lisa didn't know that every women has three avenues of love, until one day I told her a story. We were naked in bed, and I was on top of her and deep inside her as I whispered in her ear. I told her about a sinister Chinese opium merchant and his submissive concubine. I limned the scene carefully, the strange jangling music, the girl dancing before her master, naked save for her jewels. Lisa spread her legs wider and arched her back to push against me. Suddenly she moaned and stopped—her buttocks clenched tight against my hands that were squeezing them—for I had just told her how the concubine had knelt, face against the cushions, while her master prepared to penetrate her tightest portal.

I moved my hands forward so that I could raise my head and look directly into her eyes. Lisa looked at me in sudden knowledge, and in the knowledge was fear and behind the fear was trust.

I pulled out.

"Turn over," I said.

She did as she was told, and gave me her last virginity.

*   *   *

I rolled over on the towel, laid my head on my left arm and closed my eyes. From a distance, say from where Amanda and Lisa were playing, I might have appeared to be asleep. But the attitude was a lie, for my muscles were twitching under the skin and I had to fight back the effect of an involuntary surge of adrenalin.

I can remember every exquisite moment I've spent with Lisa, but it is also necessary to recall that after every interlude of love she has returned to her husband—a Legal Aid lawyer who practiced in the lower depths of Scranton, Pennsylvania.

She loved him because she thought he represented

all that was good in the world. She had almost died for him.

I hated his guts because in seven years of marriage he had never told Lisa that she was pretty.

Lisa met Jeffrey Thatcher in the fall of 1970 (the same year that I discovered Amanda) when they were both attending Swarthmore College, a small liberal institution (interestingly enough, it was founded by the Society of Friends) in southeastern Pennsylvania. This was near the height of the antiwar movement, and Lisa found her future husband sitting behind a cardtable that was set up on the lawn in front of the Student Union. The banner spread across the table announced that he was soliciting funds to send food and medical supplies to North Vietnam. The first thing she noticed about him was that his brown hair was cut unfashionably short, almost a crewcut—in fact, neither the hair nor his pointed little mustache went at all well with his broad middle American face. (She found out later that he had his hair cut each month by a Puerto Rican barber in Philadelphia. In this way he supported the Third World, while also making a statement or principle: "I'm too busy to hassle with hair over my face," he told her. "My political stance is a reflection of my actions, not my looks.") The second thing she saw was the red button pinned to his shabby black T shirt—the command was in clear white letters and seemed aimed directly at her: "Get Involved". The third thing she noticed was what decided her. Try as she might, Lisa had too much on top for effective concealment. Most men looked first at her breasts. But that was not the direction of Jeffrey's gaze, nor was he looking at her face. He was watching her hands, to see if she was going to reach into her purse for some money.

She walked straight over to him and said, "I want to get involved."

"Get a chair," he replied, barely glancing at her.

She obeyed.

I'm sure he loved her from the first, because she was always acolyte to his saint.

I wonder if he knew that when she carried that chair out from the Student Union, she was carrying the gift of herself.

Did he appreciate her when she took off her clothes for him? Or did he take her, even the first time, as one might down a hamburger at McDonald's—a quick slaking of a momentary appetite?

I don't know, for she never told me what he was like in bed (though as I've mentioned, it was clear from her own lack of experience that he was a man of simple tastes). In fact, she never spoke of him at all unless I mentioned him—whereupon she would immediately launch into a long and boring recitative of Jeffrey Thatcher's good works.

It was boring to me but not to her. Even the smallest tale of his charity—a dollar given to a street-corner beggar, a cripple helped across the street—made her eyes light up with devotion.

My right hand curled around a lump of sand and I squeezed it like a neck. I thought of Lisa announcing her own death—and I felt an almost voluptuous sense of loss in every molecule of my body. I could not imagine the course of my life had there been no Lisa to love. I jerked my head up from the towel to look at her, to reassure myself that she was still alive and breathing.

She wasn't there.

Amanda wasn't there.

I jumped up into a sprinter's crouch, heart at 120 beats per minute—and then the rational part of my brain intervened. I looked in the proper direction and saw them walking hand in hand, just two hundred yards away. They had almost reached the hut marked Facilities.

I let my breath out slowly, I let my body relax as I watched them. I wondered if they would kiss inside that dark enclosure—that was a fantasy, but I've often thought that my whole life is a fantasy: one that I have made real.

* * *

Lisa never told me the secrets of her mind until I had discovered the secrets of her body. I'll never forget the first time I undressed her—or more precisely, the exact moment when I unfastened her bra. KABOOM! Her breasts tumbled down her chest like twin waterfalls of flesh. I had never seen breasts so big in my life—not even in a magazine. (Later on I would discover that there are specialty magazines devoted to nothing but girls who look like Lisa, but at that time I restricted myself to the more conventional Playboy, Penthouse, Gallery etc.)

Well, nakedness is truth, and to tell the truth I was a little turned off by her abundance, just because it was strange. I touched one—and another surprise—her breasts were so-o soft—nothing at all like Amanda's firm ripe pears. Even a slight pressure caused my fingers to sink into her flesh—I was afraid that I would hurt her.

I made love with Lisa many times after this, and gradually I learned how to play with her breasts, to squeeze them gently toward her wide pink areolas, to run my tongue over her short pale nipples until they were hard and glistening. And as I loved the woman, so I came to love Lisa's breasts more than any other part of her, just because they were so distinctively hers.

One day in bed I told her just that—told her that her breasts were wonderful—and she gave a little cry in her throat, snuggled up against me and put her head on my chest. I cupped one of her soft breasts as she began to speak, lips almost against my skin. She never looked up at my face; she spoke in a low, level voice as she told me the story of her death.

"It was Jeffrey's last year in law school and—I just stopped. He read to me from newsmagazines every night—famine in Africa, torture in South America, slave labor in our own Southwest. He expected me to remember these things—and he got mad when I forgot the names of the dictators. A girl who wasn't even in my class passed out one day as I was overseeing a study hall. I took her to the nurse's office, and my face was the first one she saw when she woke up. She was on drugs, she didn't even know what kind. She thought I had saved her. She told me she loved me; she promised to give up drugs, and then I would get calls from her at two in the morning, 'Mrs. Thatcher I broke my promise,' she'd cry, and I'd ask, 'Where are you?' and she'd say, 'Some bar in New York.' I had a girl in my class who lived in a shack with no indoor plumbing—her older brothers treated her like some Cinderella with no hope for a prince, while they tooled around on their snowmobiles.

"I couldn't help. I couldn't move because everything was pressing on me. It was crazy because we were supposed to have a party—the week before I met you at that tournament. It was to celebrate Jeffrey's impending passage through law school—he had even invited some of his professors. And I couldn't even tell him that we couldn't do it. We were broke.

Not just broke but finished, gone under. My salary just couldn't support us and send him to school as well. He had tried for a student loan but his name was on some kind of list and he couldn't get it—I think because of his war protests. We lived beyond our means each year and now there was nothing. The toilet didn't work right, and the landlord wouldn't fix it because I had been stalling him for three months.

"I couldn't listen to another word about starving blacks in Alabama because we were dying right now. And he didn't know. He was oblivious—and yet I knew that what he was doing was right. We should get involved, we should help the oppressed, and I knew that he would use his law degree as a tool to do just that.

"I couldn't buy groceries for the party, I had never done anything in my life to be proud of ('Not true,' I said against the top of her head, but she went on) but I wanted to do this right."

I watched the girls come out of the hut, watched them slowly get bigger as they approached, while I replayed the rest of Lisa's speech in my mind. She had told me about the one bill that Jeffrey insisted on paying each month: the premium on their life insurance. He had almost died as a child (hit by a car, his knees were never completely right). I remembered that he could recite accident statistics like other people knew batting averages. He never expected to live long—but Lisa decided to go first. After all, she was worth more dead than alive.

It was a well established fact that Lisa fainted at the sight of blood. There had been humorous and embarrassing incidents at parties past.

She decided to have the accident while peeling a cucumber (she had originally thought of a roast, but then she couldn't afford it). The knife would slip—

slash through the wrist—and she would faint with her life leaking out around her. When Jeffrey returned from school with the first guests, they would find her on the floor. It would be messy and flamboyant and the only truly spectacular thing she had done in her life.

What stopped her? At the last moment, she decided not to walk willingly into the arms of death, but rather to roll the dice. She told Jeffrey of her plan.

She told me with some satisfaction that it had really shaken him—the first time she had really moved him in their marriage.

He went around to each of his professors, and he borrowed enough money from them to make it through his last semester. For a time, he was even kind and loving to his wife.

It wasn't enough. I wonder if perhaps she felt betrayed—after all, she had offered him her greatest gift and been rejected.

In any case, she was left with that raging urge to live that follows any brush with death. She had no one to spend it on—until a week later, when she met me.

I stood up as the girls came near. I put an arm around each and hugged them close.

"It's time to go home," I said.

* * *

The vehicle was a 1960 Comet, a square blue box with huge red slanted taillights. Amanda called it "my Oriental car" and she loved it, despite the fact that it steered slightly to the left and had a top speed of about 50 mph—any more and the engine started to shake apart. Some people might have described it as an old piece of junk that wasn't worth the $100 we paid for it—but to Amanda it was pure joy, for it meant the end of hitchhiking.

Amanda was driving, because it gave her such pleasure. She liked to control her life; she didn't like surprises. The long slow build-up to my affair with Lisa had not bothered her. When I came home after my first erotic weekend with her friend (the girls had met at a few chess tournaments and they had gotten along well from the start—Lisa's bright quickness was a perfect foil for Amanda's solemnity, though it always amused me to see how they reversed those roles in bed) I was a little nervous, but there was no need. Amanda wanted to hear every detail—and then we spent the rest of the day talking and making love.

Amanda hated not knowing when the next dollar was coming—it was never easy for her to deal with the fact of the loss of her childhood wealth. Each week she fought uncertainty as I went off to battle with wooden knights—would I win and come home with a nice present for her, and a bit of cash for the bills? Or perhaps I would lose, maybe only due to a blunder in time pressure, the ruthlessly ticking chess clock forcing my hand, and the foul consequence being that we would be broke for two weeks. She hated the randomness of my part time jobs, and she hated to think of the brilliant man she had married loading trucks. But the worst thing of all was simply trying to get from here to there—too many miles to walk, and you stand there, never knowing when a car will stop.

The Comet changed all that. It was possible to pick up a beautiful friend (whose husband was far too busy with his indigent clients) and drive to the beach for a day! It was possible to drive back into the sunset, listening to Lisa chirping like a happy bird as she related the plot of some forgettable TV movie. It was possible to relax, traveling at a stately 45 mph, and feel your husband's hands massaging the back of your neck. And it was even possible, within the safe confines of the car, to step inside the thoughts of the man she loved, and I felt her shiver and then sigh as she pressed back against my hands.

Lisa stopped in mid-sentence. "Are you listening?"

"I'm driving," Amanda said.

"I'm thinking," I said.

Lisa half turned to look sharply at me over the seat. "I know what you're thinking," she said.

"I'm sure you do," I said, disengaging one of my hands and putting it on Lisa's neck. "I'm thinking of the U.S. Open."

"Right," said Amanda.

"Absolutely," said Lisa. The girls looked at each other with exaggerated expressions of disbelief, and then Lisa continued, "So tell us about the U.S. Open."

"It's in Columbus, Ohio."

"That's profound," said Lisa.

"It starts in six weeks."

"Most interesting."

"Grandmasters and International Masters from throughout the world will be there. I'll be ranked about fiftieth to start with, but . . ."

"But what?"

"But I'm going to win it."

"That would be nice," Amanda said.

"Have you ever beaten a Grandmaster?"

I looked hard at Lisa and said, "That's not a nice question, but I do have an answer." I leaned forward and kissed the top of Lisa's head, and then did the same with Amanda. "No, but *now* I have inspiration."

The girls smiled, and I saw just a flash of Lisa's tongue. I leaned back like a king in a chauffeured limousine and calmly surveyed the two lovelies in the front seat. "You see, I really was thinking of the tournament."

* * *

Amanda turned the Comet slowly into the alley in front of our house. It was that last moment before complete darkness, and the local kids were still trying to play street hockey. I never figured out why they played hockey in the summer instead of the baseball I had grown up with, but then again I never asked them. The kids scattered as the car crept along—I saw the flash of a white T shirt passing quite close to a side window, but the boy himself was invisible. By the time we had reached the garage, night had fallen like a black curtain.

We piled out. I got Lisa's suitcase out of the trunk (this being her summer vacation, she was planning to stay with us for two days) while Amanda led the way to our house.

I said, "our house", but that is hardly a description that can be taken at face value. It's true that in a moment of utter madness—well, I must beware of easy explanations. We did buy the house, we did get a mortgage, and madness has never yet convinced a banker. The truth is that Amanda had prepared her move for a long time, and all she needed was the right moment. Amanda hated renting, for all the usual reasons: faulty repairs, arbitrary rent increases, surprise evictions—in short, no control. She often talked of buying a house—I dismissed this as nonsense, for of course we had no money. Nonetheless, she went on with her calculations, and in the euphoria that followed my win in the 1975 Pennsylvania Championship, she convinced me to go along with her plan. I never expected it to work, but Amanda was most persuasive.

She had it all ready when we finally got to meet Chuckles—the somewhat bizarrely nicknamed loan officer. In a speech that would have melted the hearts of the hardest jury, she explained how we would rent out the first floor, that she would continue to make good money as a waitress, while I . . . Well, 1975 was the year that Bobby Fischer was to defend his World Championship title that he had won so brilliantly from Boris Spassky at Reykjavik in 1972. A five million dollar purse had been announced for the new match against Anatoly Karpov—for just that moment in time, it seemed as though there would be a giant infusion of money into the ancient game.

The deal went through—we bought a run down house in a good neighborhood—and Bobby Fischer threw away his title, threw away the money, just hawked one colossal gob of spit all over the chess world . . . The businesses that were going to sponsor chess—with Fischer—all pulled out, and masters were left in the same penury as before. So Amanda continued to wait on tables, I worked at odd jobs and occasionally won a big two hundred dollars in a weekend tournament. There was no way on earth that we could pay the mortgage plus the repairs that continually plagued us. After two years we were just one step ahead of foreclosure. The issue was really quite simple—if I won the U.S. Open, we could keep the house. Anything less, and Amanda's dream was gone.

Amanda led the way up the fire escape (the front door was stuck permanently closed, analogous to the way the garage door was jammed permanently open) and Lisa followed her a little gingerly. I patted Lisa's ass to brush away my melancholy thoughts—she jumped and I smiled.

"Home at last!" I cried, as Amanda opened the door.

Amanda flipped on a light and asked Lisa, "Would you like something to drink?"

"Yes," Lisa answered, and then she hesitated. No stranger to money shortages, she was afraid to ask for something we wouldn't have.

I stepped into the breach. "Amanda, look in the refrigerator and see what we have. Lisa, let me show you your room."

I picked up the suitcase and carried it down the hall, turned right and flipped on another light.

I put the suitcase down. "This is normally my study."

Lisa looked at the chess set, abandoned just before the mate in Rosanes—Anderssen, Breslau 1863. I was going to say something about the position, when I noticed Lisa's eyes following the sightline from my chair past the chessboard to the wall. There I had placed (for inspiration between moves) a poster of an exceptionally attractive centerfold model. This lady, with flowing red hair and a slim, perfectly proportioned body, was a beautiful girl by any standard; and the photograph itself was exceptional. She was caught standing nude on a deserted beach, silhouetted in half light gazing out to sea. She had a stillness that was the epitome of poised eroticism.

"I don't look like that," Lisa whispered.

I put my hand on her right shoulder and turned her until she was facing me. My eyes were hard and cold when she finally looked up at my face. There was no pity in my gaze. She quickly looked down as I put my hands on either side of her face, gently cupping her cheeks. I held her for a moment, and then my hands slid slowly downward, following the column of her neck and then moving in front to rest upon her breasts. It was hard for me to feel anything through the armor of her bra but I knew how much to squeeze—and I did so—and then a little more, just enough to make it hurt. She looked up at me again, her eyes wide, and I put my arms around her and pulled her close. As her head went back she smiled and I smiled too—our lips were no more than three inches apart when we heard Amanda's cheerful call, "How about some lemonade?"

We couldn't help laughing as we disengaged and headed back to the kitchen.

* * *

"Don't you think you should save your strength?" Amanda asked.

We were lying nude on top of our single extravagance, the king size bed we had not yet paid for. Down the hall Lisa was quiet, perhaps asleep. The windows were all open; the curtains were open too, in the hope of enticing a stray breeze. I could hear the whine of a streetlight outside as its light slowly expired. I could just make out Amanda's face, her teasing expression—I had just put her hand on my rapidly growing cock, and despite her query, her fingers had already encircled me with a practiced caress.

"Do you think I need to?"

"Did you kiss Lisa tonight?"

"You saw—I kissed her good night."

"No, I mean earlier, when you showed her your study."

"Never miss a trick, do you?"

"So you did."

"I would have, but you had perfect timing with the lemonade."

"Good."

I put my right hand in her hair and moved over her until I was looking into her eyes from two inches away.

"Bitch," I said against her mouth, and then I kissed her hard. Her mouth opened for me and my tongue went in deep, as my left hand found her breast and felt its firmness. I marvelled at the difference between her and Lisa, for I could cup nearly all of this one in my hand, and her breast did not sag at all—I could feel her hard nipple scratching against my palm. I moved my hand down just a little, caressing the sensitive underside of her breast, and my thumb flicked over her nipple. Amanda moaned against my mouth—her lips opened wider and her legs spread as she tried to get all the way under me— but I wouldn't let her.

My hand was tight in her hair as I broke the kiss. She tried to reach my mouth again, and I let her have a quick peck, and then I began to force her down.

Amanda knew what I wanted, but still she resisted, stopping to plant kisses on my neck, my shoulders, my chest—and I would let her, easing my grip for a moment, only to press down hard again the second after her lips had made contact.

Finally she came to my cock, and she kissed it up and down, both sides, still teasing, still fighting, until I pulled her head back hard until her mouth opened and then slowly let her come back down. She ran her tongue over the tip—and then in complete surrender she slid the rest of the way down, taking all of my stiff manhood in her mouth.

I relaxed my hand in her hair, letting her come back to the top to breathe, and then slowly find her way back down. At the deepest point, I tightened my hand again and flexed my cock so she could feel me grow in her mouth. Then I relaxed, and she slowly moved up to the tip, as we settled into an old rhythm.

I took Amanda's pillow and put it on top of mine so my head was raised enough to see her whole body as she lay between my legs—her ass clenching and relaxing, her hard nipples rubbing against the top sheet, her face dreamy and soft beneath my hand in her hair.

Feeling the pleasure of her mouth, I reflected that there was only a single problem in the sexlife of our marriage—I pressed down hard and held Amanda there for a moment longer than usual, letting her feel the throbbing in my cock before I let her slowly rise up—that problem is that I'm a twice a day man married to a once a day woman. Amanda gives her all in bed—and then she relaxes totally. But for myself, I know that an hour after we have come tonight, I will be clear eyed and awake (probably thinking of Lisa) while Amanda will be snuggled against me, sound asleep.

My desire leads me to always want another woman in my life. I don't have men friends (a combination of egotism, cold honesty, and ruthless competitiveness makes it hard to be one of the boys) so I need another woman for balance—someone to talk to, write letters to, someone to kiss at chess tournaments and say good-by to at bus stations. Ever since we were married there has been a woman like this. Some last a year, some more, some less. I wrote many letters to each one, was fond of them all—but I never truly loved any of them until Lisa, and she was the only one I had taken to my bed.

It's interesting, but Amanda and I had fights over all of the "other women" except Lisa. I think Amanda knew that I loved Lisa before I even knew myself—I felt a sudden tenderness toward my wife, and I looked down at her face and willed her eyes to meet mine. She looked up, and I gently pulled her up and off my cock.

She came easily into my arms as I half lifted her up the bed—then I laid her down on her back and her legs fell open for me. Her eyes were glistening as I moved on top of her—and then she put her arms around me and pulled me tight as I slid all the way home.

*   *   *

It was an hour later, and I lay on my back, just one pillow under my head now. Amanda was snuggled against me, her head resting on what she called "my spot"—the soft hollow just inside my shoulder and above my ribs. The spot was a perfect fit for her head, and her hair tickled pleasantly as it flowed across my chest.

I was thinking of Jeffrey. How could I get rid of the schmuck? It wasn't going to be easy—punching him out would only entrench him further in his position of put upon martyrdom. I knew from experience that even the slightest attempt at criticism would have Lisa springing to his defense with yet another Tale of the Good Samaritan. Perhaps she would tell me again of the lost Swedish tourists whom Jeffrey had put back on the proper path. I had heard that

story three times, and each time it made me sick—
for while Jeffrey was always alert to other's troubles,
always ready with a helping hand, he never demon-
strated even one tenth of that concern for his wife.

I remembered a bizarre night (before Lisa and I
became lovers) when Amanda and I visited the
Thatchers. Lisa had kindly promoted me at the
Scranton chess club, and I had given a simultaneous
exhibition there. I took on thirty opponents at once,
each of whom had paid five dollars for the privilege
of playing a master. I didn't do particularly well,
winning 25, drawing 3, and losing 2, but it was re-
spectable—and more important to Amanda and me,
it was a much needed $150.

Afterward Jeffrey and Lisa took us to their apartment in Spirit Lake, about five miles north of the
city. We had some dinner, and then we sat in their
tiny living room and chatted for a while.

That is where the strangeness came in. Lisa and
Jeffrey sat next to each other on their miniature
sofa. They were close enough to touch—though of
course they did not. Lisa regaled us with humorous
tales of their marriage: the John Bircher who got
drunk at their wedding, a slapstick snowball fight,
their curiously dilapidated autos and so on. Jeffrey
would interrupt her narratives at various points to
get in his side of the story, and I must admit he
showed a certain dry wit.

Yet I could hardly concentrate on *what* they were
saying, so fascinated was I by the *way* they were
saying it. Jeffrey and Lisa *invariably* referred to
each other by the third person pronoun, just as if
their partner was not in the room. He or she—and
that was it. After a while it became a game. I listened
intently to see if they would slip up even once and
include the other in the conversation with a "you"

or even (Heaven forbid!) refer to their spouse by name.

It never happened. For example, a normal couple might tell of a snowball fight like this—

Wife: (turning toward her husband) You remember that night I came back to the college after a blizzard. (turns back to guests) That's when I learned how sneaky Jeffrey can be.

But Lisa said it like this, looking only at me: "I went to see him at college once after a blizzard, and you know Ray, that's when I discovered how sneaky he could be."

And Jeffrey continued, "She says I'm sneaky but if she had thought of zapping me with a snowball first, she would have."

They reacted to each other, but they never acknowledged each other.

I didn't see them together that much, but I learned enough to be absolutely certain that that night was no exception.

Why would Lisa have wanted to kill herself for a man who didn't call her by name, a man who didn't know the meaning of the word endearment? Why didn't she leave him? I couldn't understand it—but yet I could understand it, her religious need to devote herself, his remoteness which made her feel guilty and inspired more and more devotion—I could understand it intellectually but not emotionally—I could only hope to surround her with warmth, love her so much that she would never return to a marriage colder than Antarctica.

* * *

An unfamiliar sound snapped me awake the next morning—or rather, a familiar sound that shouldn't

be there. I felt Amanda next to me, sleeping soundly—
I ran my hand down her back to her soft bottom,
and squeezed a haunch gently. I kissed her hair very
lightly (so as not to wake her) for I had organized
the sounds in my mind. Lisa was taking a shower.

I lay back and stretched luxuriously. I loved the
idea of having two women in the house. I loved the
two women.

I heard Lisa getting out of the bathroom. I put on
my dressing gown and went to meet her.

Lisa was wearing a plain brown nightgown that
went with her married life—but certainly not with
this situation! She was wearing a little eye shadow
and lipstick. I smiled, seeing the make-up, for she
had never worn any in the years that I had known
her—until after our first night of love. The next time
I meet her, there was a pleasing change about her
face—Lisa told me how she had taken Stacy aside
(her pretty chessplaying student who was always perfectly made-up) and asked her how to put the stuff
on!

"You're lovely," I said.

Lisa smiled, but I noticed how she hunched her
shoulders together, with her arms in front of her—
she had not put on her bra yet, and her great breasts
lay low and soft against her body. They didn't stand
up and press the nightgown into some alluring silhou-
ette like the starlet on a Mickey Spillane book
cover—so did I care? Certainly not!

"And don't hide them," I said.

I came up to her and very gently took her wrists
and pulled them around behind me so that she had
no choice but to hug me.

I always knew when Lisa was excited because she
lost the power of speech. Her sexuality was primi-

tive—she was either all the way ready or she was not.

I moved slightly closer and put both hands on her ass.

"I like your lipstick." I looked at her mouth and her lips parted, waiting for my kiss, "But I'm not going to mess it up now. After all, you've brushed your teeth and I haven't. I'm just going to do this . . ."

I kept my left hand on her ass, squeezing her through the nightgown, while my right went down and under, lifting the material. I went up her thigh and found her cunt as wet as I imagined. I put my longest finger deep inside her and leaned still closer so as to feel her treasures.

"I love the feel of your breasts against me."

It took all the strength Lisa possessed to force her reply out, and the three words came slowly, with wide spaces between them. "I . . . love . . . you," she said.

Her blue eyes with the blue shadow above them looked like deep pools. I felt I was looking into her very soul and I saw that what she said was true. Suddenly I wanted her more than ever before—I felt my blood pumping and I drove my finger as far inside as it would go. I wanted to be against her, inside her, but there wasn't time.

The rush of the moment passed, and I felt a joyous calm over me, a calm that was a mixture of pleasure and power. I realized that with Lisa's gift of love came the complete possession of her body. I moved my left hand up her back and collected her hair into one thick handful. I took my finger out of her cunt—Lisa gave a short cry, which was abruptly cut off as I pulled her head back by the hair and presented my wet finger to her lips. Lisa opened her mouth, and tasted herself, sucking my finger like a small cock. I felt her tongue sweep over my finger as her head went back even further (as though it was too heavy to hold up) and her eyes started to lose their focus.

I gently took my finger from her mouth and held her tight, letting her lean all of her weight against me . . .

I grew up on a farm and spent most of my young life in the woods. I knew all the wild creatures by the tiny sounds they made.

I have been married to Amanda for seven years and I have known her for eight. I know the way she moves and the shape of her body. Without looking, I suddenly reached behind me and snaked my arm around Amanda's waist. Her fingers brushed my ass as I swung her around. I think she was sneaking up to goose me, but instead she was abruptly jerked through the air, ending up with her face about four inches from Lisa's.

The girls looked at each other in bewilderment for a moment, and then Amanda turned to me and said, "One of these days I'm going to catch you."

I smiled at her and squeezed Lisa with my left hand, so that she would know that everything was all right.

"Good morning, my darling." I kissed Amanda very lightly on the lips. "Would you like to use the bathroom next?"

"I think it's your turn," Amanda said with a meaningful glance downward. "Perhaps you should take a cold shower."

I shifted toward Amanda, took her hand and placed it on the swelling beneath my dressing gown. "With such beauties as you around, do you think it would have any effect?"

Amanda squeezed once, which certainly did nothing to lessen my excitement, and then she smiled a little ruefully. "I guess not," she said, and then she realized that she was quite forgetting her duties as hostess. The wheel of fortune had spun all the way round in less than a minute, and now it was time to be civilized—and help Lisa shed her embarrassment, for which there was no need.

"Good morning, Lisa," my wife said, with a propriety that Emily Post would envy.

Lisa let out her breath with a nervous laugh, and then in an exact imitation of her friend's tones said, "Good morning, Amanda."

I took Amanda's hand from its resting place, took Lisa's, and placed their hands together. I left them standing there, two civilized ladies greeting each other, while I went down the hall to the shower.

* * *

Breakfast was a comedy. Amanda tried very hard to make a simple meal of sausages, eggs, and toast. Lisa tried just as hard to help her, which considering the cramped space and unfamiliar environment, made Amanda's job twice as difficult. Meanwhile, I fell to my duties with a will: I read aloud from the salacious parts of William Kotzwinkle's wonderful book, *Hermes 3000*, and I was always ready with a pat when one of my loves bent over the stove.

Yet even in the midst of this cheerful confusion, I noticed a slight shadow in Lisa's responses. Her emotional current was slightly off kilter—I remembered that when I came out of the shower, I had seen the girls discussing something with lowered voices. So Amanda already knew—and she was as affectionate as ever, so it was probably nothing to worry about.

I read a little more Kotzwinkle—but now I was consciously aware of the small question blinking in the back of my mind: what is causing Lisa's anxiety?

It has become a characteristic of mine, since the discovery of Amanda's headaches, that whenever something is bothering my wife I want to find out immediately what it is. Blaming myself for not noticing Amanda's pain, I have become oversolicitous (prying might be a better word). I realize I'm still overreacting—and Amanda isn't that thrilled either. Often she simply tells me to leave her alone—and sometimes I annoy her so much about some small problem that is none of my business that we end up with a huge fight.

I realized that I was applying this same overreaction, oversensitivity to Lisa—I tried to ignore the shadow in the room—but I worried . . .

Would I be able to enjoy my loves together? I had discussed the idea of a menage a trois with each girl separately, and both Amanda and Lisa had agreed in principle to give it a try. They knew it was an important fantasy of mine—Amanda had fond memories of a girl-friend named Michelle from her schooldays—Lisa had never had any experience with another woman, but I think she was a little curious. So we had tentatively planned it for this weekend, though now that we were all together no one had quite had the courage to mention it.

But what was bothering Lisa? It took all my will power just to go on reading my story in the same joshing tone—for I knew to stop now would be fatal—Amanda had told me often enough about the bad side of my feverish curiosity.

There was no reason to break the easy flow of story and small talk. Amanda was happy (Miss Control hadn't even got upset when the toast burned!) and Lisa, after all, was far more happy than she was upset. I made it through breakfast—but fresh doubts kept piling into the back of my mind. Did Lisa say something that would cancel the menage a trois? Was Amanda happy that the scene was off?

My mind was strung tight as a wire. I was aching with the desire to know my two women in every way.

* * *

We were sitting in the living room, Amanda and Lisa on the hide-a-bed sofa (the bed really was hidden—the ensemble had been so badly bashed about getting it through narrow door frames that the bed would no longer come out) while I was sitting on the chair opposite. Beside me our library stretched from floor to ceiling on bookshelves Amanda had made.

Amanda was pointing out some of the more interesting juxtapositions among our books—we followed a strict alphabetical order, so *Atlas Shrugged* by Ayn Rand was placed next to a minor league prono, *The Sexy CBer*, supposedly authored by Hot N. Ready. Lisa was laughing a little uneasily—I had introduced her to hotter stuff than that, but explicit sex in black and white still made her nervous.

But there also seemed to be another worry . . .

I looked at Amanda to get her attention. Our eyes met and I let her see into my mind. After seven years of marriage we can complete each other's sentences and read each other's thoughts. I'm not a mystic and I don't think of this as strange—it's the familiar touch of a love that is known. Amanda smiled and I turned to Lisa, but before I could speak Amanda cut in.

"Raymond is going to ask what is bothering you," she said, then glanced at me to confirm. I smiled—she looked back at Lisa and continued, "And then he is going to ask what we were talking about while he was in the shower."

Lisa looked at me—back to Amanda—back to me—I grinned at her and said. "We communicate by wiggling our toes—see?" I extended my bare foot, toes wiggling for her inspection.

She smiled then, looking down, and I wondered if she would say anything about Jeffrey, about their lack of communication, but I realized again that she never mentioned him unless I brought him up, when there would come the usual fierce defense.

Now she raised her eyes from my toes and said in the saddest little voice I've ever heard, "I forgot my diaphragm."

I couldn't help myself. I said "Whew!" in a tremendous exaggeration of relief, fell off the chair, rolled over twice and came to rest at Lisa's feet. I kissed her ankle, looked up at her face and said, "So that's what you were talking about! And I thought it might be something important!

"Amanda, go get your latest Cosmo."

(Yes, I admit it. I am the sort of man who reads Cosmopolitan!)

Amanda brought the magazine, and I quickly found the ad I remembered. It featured an alluring model and a dispenser of contraceptive foam.

"Are we in business or not?" I asked, as the girls bent their heads over the picture.

They looked at each other, and then down at me, still lying on the floor.

"We're in business," they said together.

* * *

There was no one at the door when Lisa and I got back from the drugstore. We found Amanda sitting on the side of the bed; she was wearing nothing but a lacy black negligee that I had bought between rounds of a New York city tournament.

Lisa began moving as though she was caught in molasses. I put my arm around her waist and slowly steered her to stand directly in front of Amanda. I put the package of foam down on the bed, to Amanda's right. I saw my wife glance at the package, and then she took Lisa's hand in hers. She kissed the hand, and then looked up into Lisa's eyes. Very slowly she raised her hands to the top button of Lisa's blouse—and opened it.

I reached around from behind and unsnapped her slacks.

Lisa stood very still, only moving a little now and then to let us take a garment completely off. We were slow, and gentle, but very thorough—when we finished, she stood completely nude between us. Amanda put her hands on Lisa's waist and coaxed her to turn and sit on the bed—and then with a little more coaxing, Lisa lay back on the bed, but with her feet still touching the floor. I knelt down before her and gently but firmly pushed her legs wide apart. Her pubic hair was soaked, and her juices were running down her thighs. I put out my tongue, and tasted her, and then I put my mouth right over her pussy and put my tongue inside. As I licked her, I looked up past Lisa's soft spreading breasts to see Amanda caressing her friend's face with delicate, reassuring fingers.

I moved back for a moment, and broke the plastic seal on the foam dispenser. I put the tip into Lisa's vagina and drove the plunger home, sending a shot of foam deep inside her.

I took the dispenser out carefully, and laid it, along with the broken package, on the bureau.

I took off my clothes quickly and got on the bed on my knees. My cock was just inches away from Lisa's face, and she turned her head and took me in her mouth.

Amanda gave me a look of such love that I couldn't have borne it without kissing her. Our lips met almost harshly, and her mouth was open for my tongue—I knew she was tasting Lisa as I kissed her long and hard, my hands tangled in each of my love's hair.

I felt that I might die of bliss—that I might float straight through the ceiling—I knew that my knees were giving way!

I slipped away from the girls and set up two pillows against the headboard of the bed. I sat up against the pillows, my legs extended before me, one hand holding my cock pointing straight up.

Lisa had come up to a sitting position; she was looking at me, and I saw Amanda lean down to whisper in her ear, but still I heard the words clearly: "You are the guest of honor."

Then Lisa was kneeling over me, slowly lowering herself, and Amanda's hand was busy between us. For a moment they couldn't find the spot, and then I caught Lisa's hips with one hand and pulled her a little forward—she sank down slowly as her head went back just as it had in the hallway earlier. She gained a little control, and looked at me, feeling me all the way inside her—very slowly she began to rock on my staff.

Amanda looked at me and then at Lisa—then in one smooth motion she bent her head and took the tip of Lisa's right breast in her mouth. I was amazed by Amanda's calm knowledge—she did perfectly what it had taken me many tries to learn. I watched the pure sensuality of my wife sucking my lover's breast—saw her hand gently cupping the other one—felt my cock like a separate entity shuddering from the overpowering beauty of the sight—and then Lisa surprised me. She gently pushed Amanda's head away, and slowly raised herself until my cock slipped out.

'It's your turn," she said, and Amanda raised her arms as Lisa carefully divested her of her negligee.

Then it was Amanda straddling my legs, and Lisa with

a helping hand on my slippery cock—Amanda's breath caught in her throat as she felt me throb inside her— and then it was Lisa bending down, her soft lips closing around my wife's firm ripe breast. It was gentle and beautiful and lascivious beyond imagination, but suddenly I could stand the gentleness no longer and I drove the women on to their backs on the bed, naked and ready for me side by side, and I drove my cock into Lisa and thrust into her hard, stroked into her and hugged Amanda, hugged them both and then switched, into Amanda deep and hard, and then switched again, going from one to the other, not knowing, not caring, just driving towards a goal that included us all, hugging them tight with my strong arms as the explosion lifted us off the bed, spinning, floating through the circle of our completion.

* * *

Gradually the sounds of the children outside filtered into my consciousness. We lay gently entangled on the bed, a little drowsy in the summer heat. "I love you," had been said in the round, and now and again someone's hand would find a lover pleasing to touch—it didn't matter who. Smiles came up without effort and then sleepily switched off—there was peace in the room.

My cock had slipped back to its normal restful proportions.

I think the kids were playing hockey again in the alley—I could hear the scrape of the puck on the gravel—when one of the younger boys burst into song. It was an old folk song, and perhaps because it was so old, he knew only the first line.

This is what he sang, in a high clear voice: "Yankee Doodle keep it up!"

There was a split second of highly charged silence—then Lisa looked at me and started to laugh, I started laughing with her—and then suddenly the laugh caught in my throat and stopped as I realized that Amanda was laughing, I saw that she had been looking right at my tired weapon when the boy sang his perfectly timed line, a great rolling belly laugh had started deep in her body, she was shaking, then she saw me watching her in amazement and she tried to stop, tried to stop but couldn't so she cried instead, tears spilling out of her eyes as years of bottled emotions came roaring out but still the wild laughter kept coming, the laughter accelerated, heading for some pitch of hysteria, and now both Lisa and I were holding her, hugging her tight and telling her it was all right, and we caught her before she went over the top into madness and we held her all the way down, until finally she stopped, lying on her back on the bed with her mouth open, breathing in great gasps, and she looked at me with her body still shuddering and her legs apart and said, "Please—"

I knew what she wanted but I couldn't help her, not at that moment, but Lisa understood and she went down and put her arms around Amanda's waist and kissed her navel, and I put an arm around Amanda's shoulders and kissed her mouth quickly in between two of her huge breaths and then Lisa was between her legs with her mouth against Amanda's cunt—

"Please—"

And I held Amanda and felt her jerk as she felt her girlfriend's soft tongue—

"O God—"

And I let her breathe and then kissed her again and watched as she put both hands in Lisa's hair—

"Please—"

And I saw Lisa's hands go under Amanda's bottom, and I wondered if she would do what I had made her enjoy, and then I knew I was right as I felt Amanda jerk again—

"O God—"

And I knew that the finger had gone right up her backside and then she was crying again, but now the word was affirmative and she said—

"Yes—Yes—Yes—Yes—"

And I watched as she came against Lisa's mouth, came in waves that spread out from her center, waves that became ripples spreading from that dropped stone in the pond, and then finally even the ripples were gone, and she was still, with a face more beautiful than ever before—the face of someone who has seen the sun on the far side of a hurricane.

She sat up a little, and kissed me, and then she pulled Lisa up along her body and kissed her softly for a long time.

I put my arms around them, and held them both—I wished always to be able to protect their beauty.

*　*　*

Six weeks later I was going up the elevator to my hotel room at the U.S. Open. I had just won my fourth game after a brutal five hour struggle. Amanda and Lisa (she simply didn't go home after that weekend—we thought her home would always be with us) were also playing in the event—a first for my wife, but Lisa had been coaching her. It's interesting that Amanda never had any interest in the game—except as to whether I won or lost—until Lisa moved in with us. In this round they had unfortunately both lost quickly—they were probably in our room, commiserating—I was looking forward to cheering them up.

The doors opened at my floor, and I stepped past a group of chess players waiting to go down. One of them, a Southern expert named Phil whom I knew slightly, called a question to me.

"Hey Ray, how'd you do?"

"I won."

"So what are you going to do, win the tournament?"

I was surprised, because up to that moment no outsider had given me any chance of winning. Then I was pleased, for I knew well that every winner has an aura—Phil was simply the first to see it. The other players were looking a little puzzled, but Phil was grinning as the doors started to close.

I could feel my own grin starting, and I called back gaily just before he disappeared.

"Of course!"

Part III

Lucky (Amanda's Story)

Lucky is a rich chestnut color all over, except for her hips, which are white like a girl who leaves her bikini bottom on to sunbathe. I do that myself; Raymond finds it more exciting to bare my O so white behind . . .

But I was talking of Lucky. She's a beautiful Appaloosa mare, and I ride her every day that I'm home—like today, this very hot April morning. Home is the countryside of southeastern North Carolina, twenty miles or so from Hollywood East, the big studios and soundstages of Wilmington. That little port city has been New York, Los Angeles, and every place in between in these last ten years; low costs in a right to work state have shaved millions off many a film's budget.

I think about millions routinely now. There was a time when I was concerned about pennies (I kept them in a bowl on top of our bookshelf, and many a time, though I hated doing it, I bought groceries with a stack of penny rolls). Now my fee plus percentage of the gross is very rarely below seven figures.

Sometimes there are eight figures.

The money matters to me, and I take care of it. I was born rich, and then I was poor, and I never want to be poor again—and I will make sure that my sons learn the value of money.

Jason is thirteen, and today is April seven, nineteen ninety-two, so Aaron will turn ten in a week.

That means I am in the last year of my thirties, as the fan magazines gleefully point out—the character roles will be coming soon.

But I don't need to think of that now. Lucky is hot between my legs—I always ride bareback—I'll just touch her whiteness lightly with my riding corp—two feet of springy wound cord with a three inch leather tail at the end—yes, that smarts, yes, that's good now, a lovely canter . . .

* * *

Lisa left us, of course, after Raymond won the U.S. Open. We didn't need her—we only loved her. Jeffrey needed her, because she was the only one in the world who validated his exaggerated opinion of himself.

He called her and begged her to come back (after two months of sulky silence that followed her own tearful call to tell him that she was staying with us)—he caught her when she was alone, and when Raymond and I got back she was gone.

I wasn't really surprised. We had been talking of having children, raising them all together—and if ever anyone was born to nurse a child it was Lisa—but children would have made her happy, and she would rather be Jeffrey's miserable slave, bound to his false goodness forever and ever.

She's two years older than me—forty-one now—and she's never had a child, and I guess she'll never have one now. Jeffrey never wanted any competition.

I used to call her, and Raymond wrote to her for many years—but she finally told us both to stop. She didn't want to be reminded of the good times— Raymond in her deep from behind while she licked me lovingly and I stroked her hair—too nice, too sweet, too hot. She and the king of Legal Aid still live in a trailer in Scranton, doing their good deeds for the local petty criminals.

Am I cruel when I think of Lisa this way? I do good deeds myself, but they have a different character. My boys go the local public school (the private ones turn up their nose at anyone who isn't a Daughter of the Confederacy, and I can do without that, and my sons can too) but I made sure every classroom in their school got a new computer. There was a little ceremony at the school to honor my gift. The principal took my hand, and I felt his tremble.

* * *

I suddenly had to rein in Lucky, and my thoughts, because there were two girls on the path. What on earth were they doing here on the private reaches of our estate?

They waved at me as I approached. One had bright flaxen hair; the other was a dark brunette. They had very young, unsure faces—and taut, very grown-up bodies that were mostly on display. The blonde wore a thin red and white checked shirt that was tied under her breasts, leaving her flat belly with its prominent navel bare. She wore a pair of tight blue jean cutoffs below—cut off just at the level of her crotch. She had sneakers on her feet, but no socks. The brunette wore a low cut body shirt and a miniskirt that was barely longer than her friend's cutoffs, and she had socks with her sneakers.

College girls.

I waved and smiled—there was certainly nothing to be frightened of here—and in my boots, jodhpurs, and steel lined riding hat I didn't think they could recognize me.

The blond smiled now, and pulled a sign from behind her back. It was hand lettered in multicolored marker on white poster-board; it said. "FORT LAUDERDALE OR BUST!"

I had to laugh, and I pulled Lucky up next to them. The brunette still looked worried.

Spring break girls who had lost their way.

Suddenly I had a thought, and my hand tightened on the hilt of my riding crop, and my thighs tightened around Lucky so that she burst forward a few steps, frightening the girls who jumped backward on either side—my jodhpurs were soaked (and not just with sweat) where I pressed down hard against the horse—I wasn't wearing any panties—I turned Lucky around, and calmed her—the girls had come close to each other again for comfort—they both looked worried now, and well you should be, I thought—my smile was gone, my laughter was gone—my face must have looked as cold as Madame Girard's did on that long ago day . . .

Yes, I had a wonderful teacher in the ways of power.

I would never see these girls again after this day. I could help them—for a price. I enjoyed holding the whip.

I spoke to the brunette. "What are you doing here, young lady?

* * *

After my first film came out, when Jason was five months old, I got a call from London—from Michelle. She told me that she had seen me the day before on the big screen; and she had spent all this day working on her father, and her father's acquaintances in the film industry, until finally she had managed to find the right connection and get my unlisted phone number.

I hadn't heard from her since I had left Madame Girard's Academy—but I recognized her voice the instant I heard it. I told her about Jason, and said I wasn't going anywhere for a while—I asked her if she could visit.

She said she would let the nanny take care of her two children (a boy, four, and a girl, two) for a week; let her husband (a rising young Tory politician) fend for himself; she asked me what kind of connection one could make from the Concorde to North Carolina.

I told her that Raymond was playing in an international tournament in Mexico City—it would be just the two of us, and my babe.

She blew me a kiss across the trans-Atlantic wire.

I picked Michelle up the next day at the tiny local airport; we hugged and I felt her red hair, as wind-blown and tangled as ever.

"Never past ten," I whispered, and she smiled with memories dancing in her green eyes.

Jason had been sleeping when I had left him in the care of the teenage girl who lived in the next house (a mile away). He was still slumbering when we returned—I paid the girl, and sent her home, while Michelle quietly admired my handsome boy.

Then I showed Michelle the guest room; she arched an eyebrow, and I said, "Well, I didn't want to presume—" She laughed, and I picked up her suitcase and carried it around and put it in the master bedroom, a door away from Jason.

There was a private bathroom as well, which Michelle made use of—when she was done I had brought her towels from the guest bathroom. I handed them to her when she opened the door—she gave me a wicked look, and reached for Raymond's and my towels on the top rack—

I said, "Michelle!" just as sharply as I could.

She smiled innocently and asked, "Darling, whatever's the matter?" in her haughtiest British accent.

"If you touch my towels," I said, "I'm going to put you across my knee and spank you so hard you won't be able to sit down the whole week you're here."

Michelle slowly lowered her hand—just then Jason began to cry.

We both laughed, and then Michelle watched when I nursed Jason. She asked me if she could suck on the other one, just for a moment—I opened my blouse all the way and she sucked just long enough to leave me hopelessly liquid with desire.

After Jason went to sleep again I kissed her, and learned the sweet taste of my own milk—and then we discovered the number sixty-nine, and I never did spank her that week.

I still get excited remembering that moment in the bathroom, and I wish she had gone ahead and grabbed my towels, because I would have done to her exactly what I promised.

* * *

"Is this your . . ." the brunette falteringly replied.

"My husband and I own the land you are standing on, yes. Now do tell me how you got here."

The blonde cleared her throat. "We met some guys—" she tried to smile winningly, but my face frightened her and she couldn't; she barely managed to keep talking. "They said they were in college too—we're from Penn State—but I don't think they were, really, even though they said they would drive us all the way to Fort Lauderdale—"

The brunette chimed in again. "We were going to take my car, but it broke down last week and we didn't have money to fly, so we took the bus, it was slow going, we made that sign on the way and joked about hitchhiking, and then these guys—"

"They picked us up at a rest stop in Raleigh," the blonde continued. "They got a couple of sixpacks on the way—I guess we weren't too smart . . ."

I looked at her, but I didn't say anything.

"I guess that little house is yours, too," the brunette said, pointing.

I nodded. Now I was starting to understand—the "little house" was a hunting lodge that I could just see from my perch atop Lucky—Raymond and I had never used it.

"So they took you here—did they know where they were going or was it an accident?" I was worried now, because I didn't like the idea of local rednecks using our property for somewhat nefarious purposes.

"No, the blonde replied, "they had been driving around, getting drunker, getting lost, I think, and then they turned off the road onto this path, and they were as surprised as we were when we saw the little house—and then they checked it out, and said it was empty, and told us it was party time."

I was relieved that the intrusion was an accident. "Was it," I asked the brunette, "a party?"

She lowered her eyes. "I don't remember too much."

The blonde was looking at her sneakers too. "When we woke up this morning, our bags and all our money and clothes were gone." She smiled wanly, "All they left us was what we were wearing and our sign."

"What are your names?" I asked.

"I'm Julie," said the blonde, with a little better smile, "and this is Terry."

"Julie, Terry," I repeated, not giving my own name—I could see, they *hadn't* recognized me, and were too intimidated to ask who I was. To them, I was just someone older, I looked rich and I was—I was authority.

I looked the girls over as though I were Madame Girard, and I asked them, "How would you like to fly to Fort Lauderdale this afternoon, all expenses paid?"

* * *

Nigel Mynton, my first film director, had authority. It frightened me terribly to challenge him—I thought I was giving up the chance of a lifetime—but then I couldn't have lived with the other choice.

I miss Nigel. Raymond and I went to his funeral last year—an English Hollywood cowboy, now gone forever.

* * *

My father used to be afraid that I would become an actress—but his fears didn't become true until long after he died. His suicide gave me sorrow and pain to draw on my whole life long—but I was nothing more than a stiff wooden Indian onstage until a little boy's song taught me how to laugh again.

Lisa's departure hurt me, but as I said, it wasn't entirely unexpected. Once she left I took stock: I had the gift of laughter, and the ache of sorrow—and I was—I am still, though touched now by years— beautiful. It didn't take me long to decide what I wanted to do.

With Raymond's victory in the U.S. Open we had just a little extra cash. I quit my waitress job, and I went to the community theater in the little river town of New Hope, Pennsylvania, just about thirty miles south of our home in Easton.

I auditioned, and I got the ingenue part in an old romantic comedy.

One night a little nondescript man came backstage, handed me an envelope, and left without a word.

I opened the envelope, and inside was a round trip ticket to Los Angeles, and a business card that said "Nigel Mynton, Director" with a phone number.

I knew of him, of course: the famed British director of twenty worldwide film hits, at least seventy years old now, living out his days in Southern California—he had made two films a year in his youth, but now he averaged one big "event" picture about every five years. It had been four years since his last film.

I exhausted Raymond in bed that night. He sometimes complains about how I fall asleep after just once, and how he needs more—I was every seductress he ever wanted this night, and after he had come in me, with me, I put myself across his lap and told him I had been thinking bad thoughts all the time he had been taking me, and I really deserved to be spanked.

I felt his manhood jerk with fresh courage under me; he obliged me—he spanked me till I cried, spanked me until there was no trace of the actress in my responses, I well and truly hurt, my bottom was definitely rosy—and then he guided my tear-stained face down . . .

He held me tight while I sucked him, tasting myself, he held me tight as he came in my mouth, and I swallowed every drop because he told me he would spank me again if I failed.

I pleased him—he drew me up and cuddled me, and I settled into my "spot"—he fell asleep, but I did not.

I got up very quietly and called Nigel Mynton.

* * *

"I saw you one night in New Hope," Nigel Mynton said in his Beverly Hills office, "and you're beautiful, but that role was hardly a stretch. Can you really act?"

"Do you always give plane tickets to girls that you don't think can act?" I asked.

"Cry," he said.

YOUR FATHER'S DEAD STOP COME HOME AT ONCE FOR FUNERAL STOP SANDY. I cried.

"Laugh."

'Yankee Doodle keep it up!' I laughed.

"You love me."

Raymond O God yes Raymond—I looked at the director like I looked at my husband.

"You hate me."

You ran away Mother—have you found Hell yet?

"Unbutton your blouse."

I did as he ordered.

"Open it. I need to see them."

I slowly parted the halves of the silk garment I had splurged on before flying out here. I didn't know whether to be proud or ashamed of the hardness of my nipples.

"And if you were wearing a bra, what would it measure?"

"38C."

"Well, wardrobe will check that later, anyway. I just had to see if they were real. You can do the buttons up now." He watched me until I was covered again. "You've got the part; I'll go over the script with you at my house tonight. My chauffeur will pick you up at your hotel at nine o'clock."

I didn't want to think about the 'my house' part yet.

"You've never really told me why I'm here."

"It's for my next movie darling—I thought you knew—it's been in the trades." He looked at me for a moment, not unkindly. "I don't suppose you read Variety in Pennsylvania then, do you?"

I shook my head.

"You see, being a Brit, I've never done an American western. And Spike Arlen, though an American, has spent half his life playing Brits from those Roger Hamilton books." My eyes must have looked dreamy for a moment as I remembered the celluloid hero of my childhood. "Seen a few of those, have you?"

I nodded, thinking of meeting Spike Arlen in person, and Nigel continued. "So anyway, Spike and I got together, and we agreed we aren't getting any younger." Nigel grinned. "It's the theater of the beyond for us in a few years, sweets. So anyway, I asked him if there was anything special he wanted to do, something he regretted not having done yet, and he drawled, 'Get me a six-gun, pardner. I want to do a western.' And I said, 'Bloody hell, I've lived out here in your west for fifteen years, damned if it isn't time that I directed an oater. Knock a few spots off Peckinpah and Ford.'

"We found a writer, good man named James Smiley, and he wrote us a corker. It's about an old gunslinger they call Lucky, 'cause he's lived long past his prime. Comes up against the meanest scumbag since Jack Palance played Stark Wilson—and nobody gives him a chance, 'cept for a beautiful, slightly tarnished saloon girl that's fallen for him.

"And that's you, my dear."

In love with Spike Arlen! "I want the part, but—"

"You'll get second billing, and I'll make sure the studio gives you some money—if you can take direction on the set like you did here, you'll be a star the day after the picture opens."

"I believe you. I do want the part. I just can't go to your house."

Nigel smiled, and then he named a string of all the most famous, admired actresses that I knew. "They've all been to my house," he said calmly, "for one night."

"One night?"

"One night, darling. A bit of rehearsal, as it were." He paused. "Or I could get someone else."

I imagined a thousand beautiful girls lined up behind me, panting for this chance that I was thinking of refusing. I thought of Raymond—of being across Raymond's lap as his hand came down, spanking me—I *had* been thinking bad thoughts—somehow I had known it would come to this.

I thought of going home and telling Raymond.

I thought of going home and *not* telling Raymond, and him knowing.

I looked deep into Nigel's assured gaze, and I said, "Then you'll have to find someone else."

* * *

"Fly?" Julie (the blonde one) asked.

"Yes, there's a little airport near here that makes regular hops to all the important Southern cities. You might have to change once, but you'll get there in just a few hours. Better than hitchhiking," I said. "I've got some clothes that might fit you, too—and I'll give you some pocket money to make up for what you lost."

Terry, the shy brunette, understood faster than the more outspoken Julie. "And what do you want—?" she almost whispered, hesitating because she still had no name to call me.

"I want you to please me," I said. "You can start by calling me Madame."

"Yes, Madame," Julie said quickly. Terry repeated her friend, a little more slowly.

I continued in a quiet, conversational voice. "Now I want you to kiss," I said.

"What?" they cried together.

"You heard."

They didn't move to obey—they just looked at me with big staring eyes, and I didn't push them—just yet. I let my request sink in, and what lay behind my request: they were nearly naked, in clothes that left them vulnerable to any passerby should they walk down to the highway; they had no money; they were trespassing on a powerful person's property at this very moment, and I could quite legally set the police on them.

They were young and naive, but not stupid. I saw their eyes change as these thoughts went through their minds; as they realized the exact situation they had got themselves into; as they realized that my words, couched as a 'request', were actually an order.

They turned toward each other—and stopped.

"If you are to please me, then you must learn to please each other first. Now *kiss*." This time there was no doubt that my words were an order.

They hugged each other tentatively—and then Julie leaned forward and pecked Terry lightly with closed lips.

I had maneuvered Lucky so that I was just behind Julie, and to her left. Her cutoffs were so short that the bottom half of her ripe buttocks were exposed. I aimed for the crease at the top of her bare left thigh, a place I knew from experience to be terribly tender—and as soon as they broke their poor imitation of a kiss I swung with all my strength, the riding crop an extension of my will, and the thin leather tail lashed into her vulnerable flesh—the welt came up red in seconds as she screamed—I looked at the mark, and it was right there in the crease, right where I had aimed, and she would feel it whenever she moved for at least a week.

I nearly came against the wet heat of the horse's sweating back, I felt my own wet heat—Julie had turned around to face me, her mouth working, both her hands behind her now, rubbing—

I said, "My contributions helped elect the local sheriff. If you would like to spend the night in jail for trespassing, then that can be arranged." I paused, and looked over at Terry, who looked like she desperately wanted a place to hide—but knew there was no shelter. I looked back at Julie—she had stopped rubbing, she was just holding herself behind with both hands, looking at me through tear shrouded eyes. "Or, on the other hand," I continued, "You could spend the morning in my bed, and get the plane tickets and money and clothes I have offered.

"Whom do you wish to please?" I asked. "The sheriff—or me?"

It was Terry who answered. "We'll please you, Madame. Just please don't hurt us too much."

"No more than you deserve," I said. "Now as I said, I want you to kiss, but this time, Terry—"

"Yes Madame?"

"This time *you* kiss Julie—make her open her mouth—make her feel your tongue—and if you don't do it right—" I raise my riding crop—"I'll whip her again, right across the first mark."

Terry put her arms around Julie—I saw her hands tighten on the bare skin of Julie's back beneath the tied shirt—Terry pulled her close, and I heard her whisper, "We have to," and Julie nodded slightly, submissively—the roles had changed, Terry was the leader now—Terry raised her hands, coming up under Julie's hair—she lifted and smoothed back her friend's blonde locks, and so made it easy for me to see—she shook her own hair back, turned Julie slightly so they were in profile to me—she wanted to make sure I saw everything—she tilted Julie's head back, and kissed her lips, and then drew back just for a second—"We have to," she said, no louder but more forcefully, the whispered breath of the words striking Julie's closed lips—the blonde's lips quivered and parted—Terry saw her moment, and *really* kissed her friend, forced her mouth farther open with hers, it was easy now that a breach had been made—I saw Terry's tongue flash pink for a second and then she drove it deep in Julie's mouth, and pressed her lips hard against the now open mouth of her friend, kissed her deep and long, her tongue swirling and demanding inside until Julie just gave up to the kiss, let her head fall back even farther into Terry's arms, let her body arch forward and press, breast to breast, against the lovely girl who was kissing her at my order.

* * *

"I got the part!"

Raymond looked at me searchingly. "And you didn't sleep with him, but you were worried that you'd have to."

"He did try to give me that impression."

"So what did you do?"

"I told him to find someone else."

Raymond smiled, and kissed me until I could barely stand. "Then what did he say?"

"He didn't say anything for a long time. Then he came over and kissed me—"

"He what?"

"Yes, just like you." I smiled winningly at my husband. "And then he patted me on the bottom and said I'd probably kill him in bed anyway, and then he'd never get the picture made, so it was just as well—he grumbled like an old bear, and then he handed me the script. He likes to rehearse for two weeks before shooting—we do the interiors in North Carolina—I have to report there in one month—that's where I get to kiss Spike Arlen too!"

"And take your clothes off too, I suppose," Raymond growled.

"Just my top," I giggled. I felt like a teenager should feel—but I had never felt this way when I was that age, I had been so serious—now I was just silly, happy, with a crush on a movie star but really in love with my handsome boyfriend—my handsome husband, who was having the hardest time staying mad at me—suddenly he just picked me up, flung me over his shoulder, and carried me to our bed.

"Let's make a baby," he said, and we did.

* * *

The girls walked together, on the right side of my horse, as we headed back to the house. Terry stayed between me and Julie; the brunette had an arm around her friend's bare waist, as if to protect her.

It was a half mile walk back—after traveling for a while in silence I told the girls to stop by a stump that had been sawed off neatly two feet from the ground. This was about the last place we could stop before we got to the open lawn that was visible from the house. Raymond was in town, the boys were at school, but Bertha, my housekeeper, would be inside. There was no need for her to see my pleasures.

Terry and Julie looked up at me—the latter was still the more frightened—there was acceptance in Terry's eyes.

"Terry."

"Yes Madame."

"Bend over and put your hands on that stump."

She hesitated—perhaps she thought that since *she* had been obedient earlier, I wouldn't whip her—or perhaps, because she had proved her dominance over her friend, I would only whip Julie.

I wasn't about to let her cling to such thoughts. I wanted to feel her tears on my thighs, later, when she licked me.

"The longer you wait," I said, "the worse you get it."

Her whole body shuddered once—and then she turned, and bent right over, placing her hands flat on the stump. Her short miniskirt rode up, revealing tight black panties underneath.

"Julie," I said in my most commanding voice, "pull Terry's panties down to the middle of her thighs."

The blonde practically leapt to obey—she didn't want another stroke. She pulled the panties down just as instructed, and then stepped back out of the way. Terry's ass was very white, untanned just like mine.

I whipped her right across the center of her buttocks, and she gasped, but she didn't cry out. She didn't move from her position. I watched the red welt come up, and then I struck again, an inch lower.

A short cry jolted out of her and her buttocks cringed together as the second welt rose bright red.

She still didn't move to get up. I inserted the tip of my crop between her thighs, and parted her slit with the tip. The leather came away wet.

I had a sudden breath-stealing urge to give her another, but I suppressed it; I spoke to Julie: "Pull her panties back up."

Terry cried once again when the tight panties settled over the welts—and then she stood up and looked at me with tears in her eyes.

"Let's go on," I said.

* * *

I knew I was pregnant by the time we shot the last scene of my first movie. Nigel, unlike a lot of directors, always filmed in sequence, for which I was grateful. I had come to know my saloon girl charac-

ter, and love Spike Arlen in and out of character—
or at least give my old infatuation full rein—with the
cameras rolling I worshipped the old gunslinger who
was giving me a way out—when the set was struck I
listened to his stories of Clark Gable, and John Hus-
ton, and Humphrey Bogart, and accepted his kisses,
and declined his invitations . . . He would put on his
most heartbroken expression, but I found it hard to
feel pity, having observed a trio of partially clothed
starlets emerging from his trailer early one morning!

Moviemaking was fun—but it only became magic
on that last day . . .

* * *

"Bertha, these young ladies will be my guests
today, but they haven't had anything to eat. I'd appreciate it if you'd fix them a light breakfast while I
take care of this horse." I gave Lucky a pat.

"Will that be all then, Madame?"

Bertha was always very quick.

I smiled at her and said, "After you get their
breakfast, why don't you take the rest of the day
off. We'll clean up."

"Thank you, Madame," Bertha said—but she
didn't risk a smile.

* * *

The actor who played Lucky's (Spike's) foe was
called Bull in the film and his stage name was Bull
Dip. He stayed in character all the time, and was
thus cordially hated by everyone else on the set.

He wore his costume day and night—the odor alone
could bowl you over before you could even think of
drawing a gun. One day he spat tobacco juice on my

bare legs just as I was preparing for my first kiss with Spike—I stared at Bull with unfeigned contempt, but he just laughed, and said, "Too bad there's no rape scene, bitch," and then he swaggered away.

I said to the wardrobe girl, "I can't wait to see him die."

* * *

I walked Lucky (named for my celluloid hero) until she was quiet and cool, and I thought of Raymond.

After he won the U.S. Open, it seemed that he broke through into some higher, rarified consciousness of his game. He earned the title of International Master, and then finally Grandmaster. There he seemed to stop, until recently—for there was no higher title on earth than Grandmaster, save for one: World Champion.

For the past five years Raymond had been ranked in the top ten in the world (financially speaking, in the best of those years, he had made $20,000—he chaffed sometimes at the disparity between our incomes, but I always understood that he was my master in bed—when he realized, even after I had made my first million, that I still wanted him that way, it was easier for him—but I knew it still hurt sometimes) but still he couldn't get to the summit.

This year he was trying something different. He had rented a small apartment in Wilmington, and he went there every day as if for a 9-5 job—just to study chess.

He always used to study at home—with pictures of naked girls on the walls, changing with the seasons—but now he said he wanted no distractions. He doesn't even want me to visit his "office."

I wonder if he amuses himself with *real* naked girls in his office—I wonder if they suck him while he ponders his variations—

He always has more than enough for me when he comes home—I love Raymond—but I will enjoy my own pleasures today . . .

I wonder if he will become world champion.

* * *

We were trapped in the barn together. Spike was next to me, leaning against a bale of straw, his legs splayed out in front of him, blood pouring from a wound in his thigh. I looked away in panic from the blood—and stared up into the hate contorted face of Bull Dip. Bull held a .45 aimed straight at Spike's heart.

"Bleedin' to death nicely, ain't you, old man," he said. "Maybe I don't need to put another bullet in you before you watch me with your woman."

I shuddered with fear, and my breasts quivered and nearly fell out of my extremely low cut saloon girl's dress.

"You better kill me now," Spike said, "because if you touch her while I'm alive, I'll kill you."

"With what, old man?" Bull answered with contempt. "You ain't got a prayer. You ain't even got a gun. You ain't gonna have no woman either, after I've had her."

Spike seemed to smile. He reached for me with his bare left hand—and yanked the bodice of my dress down. My suddenly bared right breast burst out, hard and full for the child to come—Spike seized my breast in his strong old hand, my nipple burst out rigid between his fingers, my head went back in the desperate excitement of life in the face of death—and Bull looked at me for just a second and not at Spike's right hand that drew the concealed double-barreled derringer from his boot with lightning speed and the first shot exploded in the confined hot barn as I cried with the painful pleasure of his hand on my breast—

Bright blood exploded from Bull's shirt, and he staggered, his gun hand swinging wildly—he fell back against a beam, and stared in disbelief at his own wound—and then he slowly started to bring his gun around—Spike shot him in the forehead with the second barrel and his skull cracked like a snapped twig, and the gun fell limp from his dead fingers.

Spike looked at the corpse, and his lip curled. "You never had a chance Bull. Don't you know I'm *Lucky?*"

Fade out.

* * *

I waved to Bertha as she drove off down our long driveway, and then I came in and looked at the girls. They were eating bagels and drinking orange juice in the kitchen—standing up.

I smiled, and said. "Go ahead and finish up—I'll just make a few calls."

* * *

Two famous television critics gave the movie, *Lucky*, thumbs down. They said it had a hackneyed plot about an old gunslinger and a saloon girl with a heart of gold. They agreed (for once) that the worst scene in the movie was where the inexperienced actress Amanda Navarre seemed to have an orgasm just from the touch of Spike Arlen's hand on her breast, while a gunfight was going on around her. They said that was ridiculous and unbelievable.

Thousands of women tied up the TV station's phone lines, disagreeing.

The next day the film opened and broke box office records nationwide.

Boys on a million street corners curled their lips and practiced their line: "Don't you know I'm *Lucky*?" None of them sounded like Spike.

I was offered a million dollars for my next role, and I accepted.

We filmed in North Carolina again—during breaks I drove out into the quiet countryside. Before I left to return to Raymond I used my salary to buy a fifty acre estate.

* * *

"You're in luck, my dears," I said.

Julie and Terry looked at me warily.

"I've booked you on a direct flight to Ft. Lauderdale, leaving at two this afternoon. Your tickets are paid for—you can pick them up at the counter. I imagine a thousand cash apiece should keep you in comfort during your revels—" I smiled brightly at the girls—"and if you want to come upstairs now we can see what we can do about clothes."

They still hesitated—but where would they run? I raised my right hand, and they saw I still carried my riding corp. I beckoned them toward me with the weapon—Terry took Julie's hand, and they came over to me.

* * *

I sat on the edge of our king-size bed: "If you're going to try on some clothes, you need to get out of

your things. Strip." I punctuated the command with
a little flick of the crop, directed toward Julie.

She hastened to obey—Terry followed her, a little
more slowly.

They were athletic girls, perfect examples of contemporary style—I'm a throwback to a softer time.
Their breasts were firm and taut, half the size of
mine; their bellies were lean; one could see definition
in the muscles of their arms. I made them both turn
around, and bend over. Their white buttocks seemed
to be the most vulnerable parts of their bodies—a
sentiment accented by the weals, two on Terry, and
one on Julie.

I didn't touch them.

"You can get back up now."

They stood up again, and turned and looked at
me on the bed. My hair was dark with sweat from
being under my hat; my face showed a pleasure in
cruelty; my blouse was unbuttoned to below my
breasts, so that the soft inner curves of each could
be seen; my hand held the riding crop; my jodhpurs
clung tight to my thighs, and a darker patch could
be seen at their juncture; my feet and lower legs
were sheathed by tall black leather riding boots.

I didn't look like a movie star. I looked like the
mistress of an antebellum plantation who has just
walked through the fields in the summer heat to
check on the slaves.

"I need to get comfortable too." I raised my
booted left leg. "Julie, come over here and straddle
my leg, facing my foot." She got into that awkward,
vulnerable position, and I raised the sleek leather of
my boot between her naked thighs and rubbed it
back and forth against her spread womanhood. The
leather glistened—she was as excited as Terry—and
twice as frightened. She grabbed my booted heel for

balance, and I said, "Yes, that's the way the slaves used to do it. Hold tight to the heel, while I push."

Suiting action to the word, I raised my right foot and deliberately pressed the sole against Julie's bottom. The narrow toe spread wide her crack—the spike heel nearly penetrated her wanton cunt—I shoved hard and she flew forward off my leg, stumbling onto the rug, my left boot in her hands.

Julie righted herself, as I left my right leg in the air. "You can do this one, Terry," I said.

* * *

There are two ways for a highly sexual leading lady to prolong her career. One is plastic surgery, and the other is the body double.

I have promised myself that I will never stoop to either of those methods. When the camera comes in close on my character's bare, quivering breast, when it focuses on her hard, glistening nipple—it is *my* arousal being transmitted to the world, not a phony substitute.

Of course, as for the glistening, I have had many a wardrobe girl suck my breasts' swollen points just before the shot—I've never yet had a girl decline my request . . .

* * *

Terry and Julie were obedient. They tried on my clothes—but I never let them dress themselves. Each one had to slide the panties up her friend's thighs; had to button the other's blouse just to half cover her breasts; had to take off and put on each other's skirts—and always, halfway through each operation,

I'd make them stop, and kiss a hard breast, or soft lips, or a downy, dripping sex.

I made sure they stayed constantly aroused—I never let them come.

They got seven outfits apiece. I watched them, naked again, pack the clothes in two small suitcases that were a bit worn; then I left them and came back with twenty hundred dollar bills.

I always liked keeping cash in the house—it helped me forget the penny rolls.

I put a thousand dollars in each girl's suitcase, and then I zipped them up, and put them on the floor behind the bed.

I unbuttoned my blouse all the way and tossed it off. My breasts swung hard and heavy toward the girls. "Are you ready to earn your money?" I asked.

* * *

I was sitting back against two pillows that leaned against the headboard of the bed, my legs spread in a moderate V. Each naked girl straddled a jodhpur clad leg; their wet sexes humped my knees as they nursed at my breasts. The riding crop was in my hand, and I flicked their reddening buttocks with the tip whenever it pleased me. They squirmed under the light lashes; they wrapped their legs around mine and rubbed hard, trying to come; they moaned around my breasts and sucked harder, my breast-flesh filling their mouths, my nipples swollen so as to seem to want to give milk—

I pulled them back off me by the hair.

They looked up at me in shock, their own impending climaxes abruptly curtailed; they looked again in fear, for my eyes were wild and the riding crop was still in my hand—

I took a deep breath, and tossed the two pillows that I had been leaning against onto the center of the bed.

'Put your bellies over those," I said. "I want your asses to be the highest part of you."

They obeyed.

I looked at their twin cleft white bottoms, streaked with red, and I remembered Madame Girard and a yellow cane on a mahogany desk—

I waited, breathing heavily, and I saw Terry's hand reach out and take Julie's and hold it tight— and then I struck, struck Terry's behind with all my force, struck her an inch below the first two marks I had given her, struck her just above the tops of the thighs, and as that mark came up I struck Julie in the same place.

I gave them each six more, of the very best.

As their hands twined together, jerking with the aftershocks of pain, I slowly shed my jodhpurs.

I stood naked away from the bed, crop in hand, and I called to my girls.

They came to me weaving, gasping, and crying—I took their hair in my hands and made them kneel.

Terry in front of me.

Julie behind.

"Lick me," I said, "both places, and make it good or I'll use the crop again." I brushed the leather against each whipped bottom in turn, a warning, and then Terry buried her face in my warm wetness, and Julie sobbed once and spread my cheeks and then I felt her tongue in that secret place, and I held her there with one hand in her hair, tossed the crop away and pulled Terry even closer as well, felt her licking, a slave licking, I bucked between them and came—

And then again—.

And came again, shuddering, and my knees gave way and I sank all the way down, kneeling between the two kneeling girls who had given me such pleasure.

* * *

I pulled the Rolls Royce to a stop far out in the parking lot of the little airport, far away from prying eyes.

The soiled outfits the girls had slept in and worn this morning seemed hardly suitable to wear to the plane—and Julie's cutoffs especially were far too tight for her to wear now—so I had given each girl one more traveling ensemble—just three items: high heels and minidress. Neither girl could even think of pulling panties on over her welts—with all three of us in front I had watched them squirming all through the drive.

Their squirming had excited me again, thinking of what I had done to cause it. I turned the car off, turned toward Julie, and said calmly, "Get down on your knees. I want to feel *your* tongue in my sex." She slipped down as I raised the short dress, similar to the girls', that I was wearing now, and then I said to Terry, "Come close so that I can kiss you."

She came willingly, and I gave her my tongue in her mouth as I felt Julie's in my nether mouth, felt her kissing that hot wet mouth and I was close immediately, I thought I was getting like Raymond, once was not nearly enough, I thought of that handsome rod that Raymond would put where Julie was licking now and I bit Terry's lips and came, bucking hard against Julie's mouth.

I fell back away from the girls, my head too heavy to hold up—I just lay back against the leather upholstery as Julie got up from her cramped kneeling position—she saw me slip unconsciously into the pose from *Lucky* when Spike had made me come with just his hand, yes the critics were right, the blood was fake but my climax was real—

"My god, you're Amanda Navarre," Julie said.

Terry looked at me in wonderment, "Yes, you are, aren't you?"

I could hardly move, this last climax had left me so weak, I just said quietly, "Yes darlings, I am."

"Can I have your—" Julie began, and then she stopped, realizing how absurd her request sounded after all we had done together.

I smiled at her. "When you sit down, any time this week, you will remember me. When you wear my clothes, and notice that the bust is too full, you will remember me. When you see me on the big screen, or on the television late at night, you will remember me." I looked over at Terry. "And I will always remember two girls who suffered to give me pleasure, who never knew till this moment that I loved them, though I will never see you again."

I looked at the tears starting in their eyes, and I kissed them both, lightly on the lips, and then I said, "Go now, or you'll miss your plane."

Terry said, "We'll never, ever forget you Madame."

"Remember me as Amanda," I said, and they smiled, and left the car.

I watched them walk away toward the terminal, each with the little suitcase I had given her in hand, my minidresses dancing in the breeze near the tops of their thighs.

Julie had to reach back and rub her bottom once before they went through the double doors and disappeared.

* * *

I picked up the boys at three, and not long afterward Raymond came home, looking very satisfied and full of himself.

He picked up a lad with each hand and swung them around.

"I think I've figured out how to beat Kasparov!" Raymond proclaimed.

Gary Kasparov was the world champion.

"That's wonderful!" I said. "And did anything else interesting happen?"

He shot me a look, and set the boys down.

"That's interesting enough, isn't it my dear? And by the way, how was *your* day?"

I had to fight to keep from laughing. "Nothing special," I said. "I rode Lucky."

The boys started dragging Raymond outside to help them catch a frog. He let them lead him out, but he gave me one more look before he left.

I didn't really think he'd believe me.

I knew we'd sort out the day's adventures, together, tonight, in our well used bed.

Sundancer

Briony Shilton

"Right. In future you will do PRECISELY what I tell you, and no more. Understand this—you have no name until I give you one. You have no possessions unless I give them to you. Your body is not yours, but mine. If I wish to thrash you daily, I will. You will not fight but accept without screaming for mercy. You will scream. I shall not feel I have done the job properly unless you do, but you won't plead or say no. Do you understand? I cannot control your thoughts, no doubt they are full of hatred for me at the moment! You hate me all right, but in time, in time you will hate your boyfriend more, for he knew what he was handing to me when he signed the contract. Long have I wanted to initiate someone into the joys of submission!"

BLUE MOON • 125 • (CANADA $6.95) • U.S. $5.95

the Tangerine

anonymous

A dreamlike tale of erotic pursuits by lovely young English ladies at the turn of the century. Whether aboard the yacht, The Tangerine or in their own abodes, all traits lead them to pleasure and amusement.

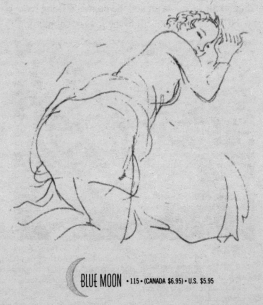

BLUE MOON • 115 • (CANADA $6.95) • U.S. $5.95

BLUE MOON BACKLIST TITLES

ANONYMOUS

#82 BLUE VELVET   **$4.95**
Trapped in a Victorian Story of O, Clarissa was trained at her father's knee and her husband's hand to endure everything. But when still others come to take charge, Clarissa turns her power to please into a weapon.

#43 THE CAPTIVE   **$5.95**
When a wealthy English man-about-town attempts to make advances to the beautiful twenty-year-old debutante Caroline Martin, she haughtily repels him. As revenge, he pays a white-slavery ring £30,000 to have Caroline abducted and spirited away to the remote Atlas Mountains of Morocco. There the mistress of the ring and her sinister assistant Jason begin Caroline's education—an eduction designed to break her will and prepare her for her mentor.

#98 CAPTIVE II   **$5.95**
Each young woman taken by the agents of Rio 9 to the remote and well-guarded estate of Camba Real pays the price of her arrogance or hostility. The *Captive II* carries on where *The Captive* left off.

#123 THE CAPTIVE III   **$5.95**
The Captive III, the Perfumed Trap, is the story of slavery and passionate training, described first-hand in the spirited correspondence of two wealthy cousins, Alec and Miriam. The power wielded by them over the girls who cross their paths leads them beyond Cheluna to the remote settlement of Cambina Alta and a life of plantation discipline. On the way, Alec's passion for Julie, a golden-haired nymph, is rivalled by Miriam's disciplinary zeal for Jenny, a rebellious young woman under correction at a police barracks.

#57 EVELINE II   **$4.50**
In this sizzling sequel, she attempts to escape the boredom of marriage by "converting" other young ladies to her wicked ways.

#19 GREEN GIRLS   **$4.95**
A superb rendition of how well a willing girl can fare at school.

#100 HARDCASTLE   **$5.95**
You are young, strong and beautiful, Astrid Cane is told, when in the sensuous and knowing hands of Lady Julia Tingle she is brought into the "full" domain of womanhood.

#93 PAMELA **$4.95**
Pamela appeared so alluringly innocent that she had no difficulty at all in acquiring the post of governess and tutor to the daughters of Sir Richard and Lady Bromley at their country estate.

#96 RETURNING HOME $5.95
The dreamily seductive Jenny returns home after a long absence to find her household replete with possibilities of pleasure. Variously coy and domineering, Jennie indulges in her most elaborate fancies.

#116 ROMANCE OF LUST $9.95
The four volumes of *The Romance of Lust* were first issued between 1873 and 1876. They comprise perhaps the best and the longest erotic novel in existence. *The Romance of Lust* is the witty first-person account of the sexual education of Charlie Roberts, perhaps the most famous hero of the Victorian underground.

#122 THE VICAR'S GIRL $5.95
In a sedate, rural village in late nineteenth century England, the beautiful Vanessa lived quietly with her brother until the day the lustful local Vicar took her in hand. From then on the proud mistress succumbed to a torrent of pleasure her body had never before known. In time, the modest hamlet became a hotbed of

passion, as Vanessa turned her new-found skills to luring other households into their secret coterie.

#31 WEEKEND VISIT $4.95
Here is another volume in perhaps the most famous erotic series of Victorian England, *A Man With A Maid*. In this sequel, Jack's life takes another fortunate turn when he makes the intimate acquaintance of his deceased friend's daughter, her beautiful mother, and their charming 18-year-old companion.

CELESTE ARDEN

#67 FANTASY HUNTERS $4.95
A crack team of bawdy women are instructed to delve shamelessly into the dark and secret world of male sexuality.

ELIZABETH BENNETT

#126 THE AFTERNOONS OF A WOMAN OF LEISURE $5.95
Joanna is a beautiful young woman of leisure. She is married to a bank president much older than herself, and is mildly dissatisified with her life. The situation is made worse by the fact that her husband no longer seems interested in sleeping with her, and by her own ongoing confusion about

herself. Several chance encounters shock Joanna into action. She becomes involved with a mysterious "O", a woman whose clients and employees experiment with pleasure, pain and what the director refers to as "issues of control". Joanna's experiences with "O" are exciting, but also dangerous. Identities are revealed, alliances shifted and plots undertaken. Joanna begins to gather secrets and to lay the foundation for her terrible revenge: graphic, erotic and ultimately murderous.

P.N. DEDEAUX

#127 ALGIERS TOMORROW $5.95
The two rich English girls were hot as firecrackers and spoiled as fallen fruit. All of North Africa knew them as The Breast and The Buttocks. Swarthy Lotharios threatened each other with murderous blades for a single chance at their bountiful white flesh, and all the while, the riotous young girls were making the local ladies of the night look like refugees from an Algerian medicare line. Britain had given them culture, and before they left, they almost proved that Britannia Rules...until they ran afoul of white slavery.

#45 CLOTILDA $4.50
Beautiful, blond Clotilda is the acme of English girlhood as we follow her misfortunes through centuries of pain mingled with pleasure, of ecstasy with agony, from the Roman conquest where she was sold as a slave to the 17th century, where she receives a birching from her Victorian curate father.

#44 THE PRUSSIAN GIRLS $4.95
The time is the early 18th century, in a Prussian ladies seminary, where the most vigorous rules pervade, providing corporal correction of its high born pupils and also its mistresses.

#61 TRANSFER POINT-NICE $4.50
Victoria and her school chum Joy, broke on the Riviera, soon find themselves being shuttled from the custody of a depraved dwarf in Nice to the clutches of a lecherous Arab in Algiers.

EDWARD DELAUNAY

#81 BEATRICE $4.95
A young Victorian woman portrayed not as a cardboard cut-out figure, but seen with all her nuances of shyness and hesitation of desires, Beatrice enters the strange fires of "love and obedience".

#112 BETWEEN THE SHADOWS AND THE LIGHT $5.95

Never was a stranger, more poetic or more powerfully sensuous novel created in the Victorian genre.

#113 DANCING FAWNS $5.95

Fresh from strict but loving care of her headmistress at boarding school, Elizabeth returns home to find an impassioned lover eager to school her further in the delights of the flesh.

#115 THE TANGERINE $5.95

A dreamlike tale of erotic pursuits by lovely young English ladies at the turn of the century.

WILMA KAUFFEN

#101 VIRTUE'S REWARDS $5.95

A green-eyed voluptuous blonde barely makes ends meet as she turns her boss' dental practice into a huge success, then becomes a porno star. It seems that the kinder and more generous she is to men, the more humiliating punishment she suffers. It's her fate to be "spanked for being good". From the author of Our Scene.

MARIA MADISON

#78 THE ENCOUNTER $4.95

She enacts the total role of being submissive, following his detailed instructions and being punished if she does not. She is beautiful and ultimately masters the "arts" which please him. From the author of The Reckoning

#117 WHAT LOVE $5.95

She is thirty, a college instructor quietly married, quietly divorced, alone now, lonely. And then, on the street one night, "I don't notice the man at first, he's like a shadow…a phantom…leaning back in the autumn twilight." And then, when she says "I'm a nice English girl", he says, "I think you've played the good girl for too long, you offend me…you're a naughty girl. Watch out I don't spank you again." She thinks, "I thought only men felt lust. It's animal, it has no conscience. It craves, it hungers. Just like me…This kind of cruel sex is my sin, my guilty secret."

RICHARD MANTON

#114 DEPARTURE FROM THE GOLDEN CROSS $5.95

This story takes place behind the locked doors of a girls' reformatory to reveal the scandalous escapades of zealous reformers and their wards.

#56 ELAINE COX $4.50

A classic study of obsession in a world of schoolgirl uniforms and correct behavior.

#111 GARDENS OF THE NIGHT $5.95
Casting aside reserve, pride and "good sense", Lesley submits to the perverse demands of her Machiavellian lover Anton.

#09 LA VIE PARISIENNE $4.95
Shuttered rooms of exclusive finishing schools...masters and mistresses matched in their perverse sexuality.

#83 LESLEY $4.95
Lesley makes a strange, dreamlike journey to a beautiful summer villa in Florville. Under the expert guidance of her mentors, Lesley gives herself over to total sensual abandon.

#110 NOREEN $5.95
A novel of obsession in the tradition of the best-selling *Elaine Cox*. Its narrator reveals his sadistic passion for Noreen, "a strapping young trollop" of nineteen.

#64 THE ODALISQUE $4.95
In the high noon of Victorian empire, Lady Jenny Langham accompanies her soldier uncle from the luxuries of London to the Nile city of Khartoum, where Jenny and her maid fall into the hands of the victorious Mahdi and spend long, hot months in erotic captivity.

#89 TRAVELLER'S TALES $4.95
Sensual adventures abound in this unique collection of excerpts from the lustiest Victorian novels illustrating the sexual practices of the harem. They vary from the Dey of Algiers' toying with British "love slaves" to the sensual surprises in the Harem of Sheikh Atra Amani.

#86 TROPIC OF VENUS $4.95
Captian Charles de Vane, educated at Oxford, was in the Army list of 1899 as an officer in South Africa. The military adventures of this gentleman took him to the far reaches of the earth—and to the exotic climes of the most exquisite sexuality.

#118 A VICTORIAN SAMPLER
Edited by Richard Manton $5.95
A masterly collection of Victorian erotic literature, from *My Secret Life* to newly discovered gems such as *Birch in the Boudoir* and *The Days at Florville*. Also included is the best history yet of Victorian erotic literature, the true story of Charles Carrington, the underground publisher of the period, a story as exciting as his books.

#47 VILLA ROSA $4.50
In the final banquet years of a decayed society, three men share a summer's pleasure with their chosen girls.

AKAHIGE NAMBAN

#15 WOMAN OF THE MOUNTAIN, WARRIORS OF THE TOWN $4.95
The adventures of Satsuki, a sophisticated courtesan of 17th century Japan, as she and the beautiful blonde prisoner Rosamund persevere through sensual and bloody adventures. A further tale in the legends of the shogun's agents.

#49 SHOGUN'S AGENTS $4.50
After receiving special rank in the Shogun service, Jira and Geoman's adventures take them to every corner of 17th century Japan and the farthest reaches of erotic delight.

#70 TOKYO STORY $4.95
Two brothers, Jim Suzuki and Andy Middler, seek the solution to the mystery of their parentage and discover a whole new world of exotic pleasures.

#95 MASTERS OF CLOUDS AND RAIN $4.95
Andy Middler and Jim Suzuki continue their search for the mysterious Cloud and Rain Corp. The two young men travel through rural Japan looking for answers, and find them in strange and sometimes very erotic ways.

#119 YAKUZA PERFUME $5.95
More erotic adventures of Jim and Andy, two Japanese American brothers who are surprised by a female agent of the Clouds and Rain Corp. who seeks refuge with them. After she leaves they are accused of stealing the secret of the sexually intoxicating pheromone perfume that is the basis of the company's power.

JAY PARINI

#66 THE LOVE RUN $4.95
Maisie Danston, a rich, sensuous Dartmouth senior, is at the moist center of this "fast-paced, lucid, sexy novel". —The Times of London

MARTIN PYX

#58 AUTUMN SCANDALS $4.95
Mona's orgiastic breach of her sorority's dating ban earns her extra retribution.

#124 SPRING FEVERS $5.95
"On our weekends, my husband and I play at being 16 year-old cousins."
Continuing the tale begun in *Summer Frolics* and *Autumn Scandals*, adult role-playing games spice California lives: Professor Porter and swamp spitfire Lucretia Sue ad-lib aphrodesiac punishments required by British-bred enthusiasts of the rod; identities blur as Lady Mildmount from *Thomasina* and

An English Education's Jane Eyre retrain a Victorian sex education truant; Sigma Epsilon Xi's toastily paddled sorority hopefuls vie to become pledge princess and weary Hollywood superstar Honey Fitz Sullivan refreshes herself with incestuous siblings, while the curse of a Goddess worshiper falls upon her unchaste son and his deceived concubine.

#52 SUMMER FROLICS $4.50
By the steaming Persian Gulf, the eunuch who read Hemingway teaches Lucretia Sue the ecstasy and anguish of unendurable pleasure indefinitely prolonged. Juliana, wife to the English consul, discovers the pangs of the White Woman's Burden in an Arab sheikdom.

#30 THE TUTOR'S BRIDE $4.95
A sun-scalded Caribbean isle welcomes New England bride Dolly Hunter. Both sexes delight as she explores local fusions of casual French libertinage and correct English discipline.

DAVID REDSHAW

#75 BITCH WITCH $4.95
Set in 18th century London, this is one of the most unusual tales of domination. Elizabeth Anderson, a dominatrix of old England uses every trick in the book. From the author of *In The Mist*

LAURENCE ST. CLAIR

#53 ISABELLE & VERONIQUE $4.50
Manhattan, Paris, London and Rome are the settings for this modern erotic triangle. A sophisticated story of intrigue and passion.

BRIONY SHILTON

#125 SUNDANCER $5.95
In this contemporary story, Sundancer, so named by her captor, is deserted by her boyfriend in a strange hotel in a strange city in the care of a little grey man, who transports her to his house as his prisoner. She is held there under a both physically and emotionally hypnotic eroticism. Punishment and care alternate until an ultimate violent awakening.

JACK SPENDER

#45 PROFESSOR SPENDER AND THE SADISTIC IMPULSE $4.50
Hired to teach amoral sorority honeys in the French Riviera sun, Professor Spender regiments their heedless sexual frolics under the brooding, lustful shadow of the Marquis de Sade.